KERRY NIETZ

MASK

MASK: AUTHOR'S PREFERRED TEXT by Kerry Nietz
Published by Freeheads
www.kerrynietz.com

Cover Designer: Kirk DouPonce
Editor: Jeff Gerke
Interior design: Mountainview Books, LLC

Library of Congress Cataloging-in-Publication Data
An application to register this book for cataloging has been filed with the Library of Congress.

International Standard Book Number: 978-0-9971658-3-8

To G'Pa Curry

For being a last minute sci-fi hero

OTHER WRITINGS BY KERRY NIETZ

FICTION

DarkTrench Saga:

A Star Curiously Singing
The Superlative Stream
Freeheads

DarkTrench Shadow Series:

Frayed

Peril in Plain Space:

Amish Vampires in Space
Amish Zombies from Space

"Graxin" (short story)

But Who Would Be ~~Brave~~ Dumb Enough To Even Try It?
(contributor)

Mask

NONFICTION

FoxTales: Behind the Scenes at Fox Software

ACKNOWLEDGMENTS FROM 2013 EDITION

To Jeff Gerke, Morgan Busse, and Jill Williamson, for your encouragement and prayers during the travails of revisions.

To Leah, for caring enough to listen, amidst the clamor.

To occasional sparring partner but incessant friend, Marc Schooley. I think, at least, in the theme of this account, we can agree.

And to the Lord, for questions and answers.

ACKNOWLEDGMENTS FOR THIS EDITION

To readers Gretchen Engel, Matthew O'Brien, and Tracy Ricard, who collectively made this a much better book than it was before. Extra kudos to Matt for finding things even Quantum would miss.

And to Kirk DouPonce, for again forming the mask.

I am the mask. The mask is me.
When others miss, I must see.
My mission just, my motive pure.
I uphold the system, the vote ensure.

CHAPTER 1

I am the mask. The mask is me.

No collector is known by name. Nor by face. There is only the mask. A dark shroud over my features. Eyeless, mouthless. Solid. I get the call, I dress, and I collect.

In reality, I'm Radial Crane. Thirty-years-old, single, childless, with a small place in the city. But here, now, I'm what I'm supposed to be. An incon collector.

And I'm waiting.

I'm hunkered in an alley off Broad Street. One hand on the cold pavement, another against the building to my left, which is slick with moisture. It is nearly midnight. The four-story building across Broad contains my target. It is an older stone structure, in marginal disrepair. A perfect place for hiding out.

Around the periphery of my vision the mask paints data—distance ranges, ambient light and temperature readings, air quality—a buffet of information.

"Hall cameras confirm the incon is present. Second floor." Quantum's voice is female, warm and assuring. That's ironic, really, since she's a synthetic brain hidden somewhere in the city. The source of all my collections. "Make good your charge."

I stand, adjust my belt, and pull on my gloves. I free two monitors from their moorings at my sides. The monitors are disk-shaped, flat black in color, and light as a hummingbird. I touch their activation spots and release them. They drop a few centimeters, and—with a slight hiss—their engines engage. They right themselves and rise to hover near my shoulders.

I nod. Inside my mask, I see the images from their embedded cameras. I now have more vision than God intended. Not quite the visual capabilities of a housefly, but almost.

With a whispered command, I send the monitors forward. They whisk across Broad and wait. I check that the way is clear and cross over behind them. Stairs lead to the front door, so I ascend. The door is metal, triple locked. To the right is a vidscreen showing the building's occupants. That is useless to me. The incon is staying with his girlfriend, and even *her* name is false.

"Security, Quantum," I whisper. Seconds later, I hear the door click open. Every building has a centralized "free" code. Originally that was for emergency services. Still is, by law.

My work supersedes all that.

I grab the door handle and crack it open. The monitors slip through the opening. I engage the eye sensor of my mask and use it to guide the monitors forward. Mostly what I'm looking for is interlopers. I don't need any complications. Often this particular flavor of incon has help. Fellow malcontents.

The building's interior is a mess. Scrawls of graffiti on the walls, most of it illegible or misspelled. The floor is littered with broken and missing grey tile.

The monitors search until they reach the first flight of stairs. They are wooden and old. There are large cracks in the stairs themselves. Places where one might fall through. My suit adds a fair amount to my weight.

I instruct the monitors to separate. One immediately takes a higher orbit, splitting the image. They make their way to the top, scanning opposite directions. I see no one, not even a hall squatter. All is quiet.

I enter the building, return the door to its closed position, and walk quietly forward. The building is said to be largely unoccupied—only twenty people amidst a city of millions. All incons or incons in the making. Regardless, I don't want to wake anyone. Complications.

I tell the monitors to make a full sweep of the second story hall, checking every door, searching for any hiding place. They find nothing.

I slowly ascend the stairs, mindful of the weak spots. There is no hurry. I have all night.

"What room?" I whisper.

"204," Quantum says.

At the top of the stairs and on my right is a door marked *201*. There is an unmarked door that I assume is 202 on my left. I slide to that wall and work my way down it. I pass the anonymous door and continue.

I pause at the edge of the door marked *204*. It is solid hardwood. Too secure for the age of the building. I check the square lock below the handle. It is an electrified thumb pad. Another upgrade. Top of the line, in fact.

Frowning, I reach for the oval decoder at my hip. I raise it and sweep it over the lock. It flashes red. I scowl and sweep it again, slower this time. I get green and hear the lock click free.

Success.

There is an explosion, and a hole appears in the center of the door, centimeters from my chest.

Swearing, I spin left, and take a crouched position. So much for not waking the neighbors.

"I don't know who you are!" a deep voice says. "But that's only a warning. Leave now, and you won't get more."

I check the images of the monitors, still poised at opposite ends of the hall. No movement from the other tenants. Not even a cracked door. They know enough to stay uninvolved. No sense pushing your own status into the red.

Plus, they probably hear gunshots all the time.

In actuality, the incon made my job easier. With a nod, I relocate one of the monitors, bringing it to the edge of the door hole, then through. I hear a string of curses followed by the *thump-thump* of quick movement. I smile, adjust the black trankers that surround my wrists. Stand.

Wait.

Though the monitor is on hi-evade, I can glimpse images as it moves. There is a dirty green couch, a smeared vidscreen, an attached kitchen, and an inner hall. The incon is crouched within that hallway. He has a table upended in front of him. His eyes are darting after the monitor. Trying to aim the silver weapon he holds. He's a large man. Shaved head. Tattoos.

Real ugly.

But is he alone?

I send the other monitor in. Shortly after it enters, there is a second gunshot. The shot strikes next to the first. The door hole is gaping now, plus the wall opposite the door is shredded. Good shot.

"Emergency calls have been made by other occupants," Quantum says. "No additional authorities have been enlisted."

No *additionals* are needed.

More movement within. Confusion. I hear a woman's shrill scream.

I shake my head. He *isn't* alone.

I put the monitors in buzz mode which only adds to the chaos. As the monitors swarm, the incon's head is darting. Meanwhile his gun hand is twitching. Looking for a shot. The woman is…

I reorient the monitor eyes. Search. I see a glimpse of hair above the kitchen counter. The next pass shows her eyes peering. Wild and white.

Have to watch for her. Watch her closely.

The incon takes another shot and hits the ceiling this time. The apartment above is unoccupied, Quantum tells me. Still, this can't go on.

I crash the door. Hit the floor. Roll right.

Another shot.

I scowl and bring the monitors closer to his head. I slide left, raise my right arm—my right tranker. Juice it. The projectile slices through the air, impacting the front of the table. Sticks. Not good.

The woman screams. I hear her crash into something behind the kitchen counter. Glass shatters.

The man crab-walks back and turns, escaping up the hall. A door slams.

"Emergency exits?" I ask.

"One," Quantum says, "But it is risky. A leap through the window."

I hesitate, wondering if I should check on the woman first. I'm supposed to. Supposed to attend to any civilians. I hear her whimpering from the kitchen. Still watching the hall, I take a step her direction.

Something collides with the side of my mask. Something *she* threw. A hard plastic cup. It doesn't hurt. Simply annoys. Now I purposely walk to the kitchen counter. Take a look over it.

The woman, Hispanic in appearance, is sitting with her back against the wall. At the sight of me she heaves another drink container. Spits.

"The vote?" I ask Quantum.

"For the woman?" she asks. "Calculating…"

"Add mine," I say.

"Recorded."

I raise my left arm, point it her direction. She gasps. I fire the trank. She shrieks as the missile hits her. Then she's down and out.

"Night-night." I say and turn for the hall. I walk cautiously past the upended table.

"Drones show he is trying for it, Collector."

"The exit?" I frown, quicken my pace. "Crazy incon."

I reach the end of the hall. There are two rooms. The door to the left stands wide open. It is a complete mess. Stacks of paper and slickzines. A dirty net access machine in one corner, keyboard stacked atop it as if to protect it from whatever rodent infests the floor. There is a reek of contraband substance.

The rightmost door is closed. I think about summoning the monitors, about borrowing their eyes again. Perhaps I can get them outside and around the building.

The exit window must be on the wall opposite the door. If Quantum is correct, the incon is poised there already. Climbing his way out.

He still has a gun…

I hear a heavy scrape, like a piece of furniture sliding under someone's weight. More breaking glass. He's not pointing a gun at the door right now, that's for sure.

I smash in, crouch, find the target straddling the window. His gun hand is down, but he quickly reacts, trying to aim.

I don't give him time. I fire another trank, catch him square in the shoulder.

The guy is like a rhino, though. He grunts, makes a futile swipe at the embedded projectile, and manages to bring his gun up. "You're nothing more than a butcher, Mask," he says. "A well-heeled butcher."

I see his finger squeeze, so I give him another trank. This time, I find that space between his eyes. He lunges, manages to fire low. Then the frame of the window breaks free. He falls back.

There's nothing I can do. Seconds later, I hear a thump.

"Incon disposed," Quantum says.

I frown. I don't approach the window. Don't even bother to check. "I know," I say. "Chalk it."

"Collection complete, Radial. Well done."

CHAPTER

Dark grease flows down the red tile wall in front of me. Between me and that wall is a five-meter by ten-meter grill. Stainless steel, aside from the black, metal grates. All of it in need of cleaning. All of it holding fragments of some dead animal. Currently there are four steaks, two chicken breasts, and a bratwurst residing there. All neatly aligned. The smoke of their cooking billows into a large vent above.

Grease coats my face and hands. The heat of the grill keeps the front of my body constantly warm. In my right hand is a wood-handled pair of cooking spats. The spats have tines like a fork and two surfaces that can be brought together over the steak. Sometimes I ding those layers together to keep myself awake. Like a mini alarm.

The hostess, Lanky Ann, brings me an order on a slip of paper. It is smeared with grease too, but that doesn't bother me. Lanky is the most figure-less female I know. Friendly. Dependable. But lanky.

Plus she never smiles. Odd, because everyone should smile in a utopia, right?

"Two tops, Radial," she says, then returns to her order desk. Beyond that is a straight line of hungry customers. All being polite. Friendly. Waiting.

To the right of Lanky the line makes an L past our selection of drinks and salad. There is no bread, of course. No dessert. The polite customers make their way past those items to the cashier. From there they venture off into our dining room, where they can eat, talk, and politely wait. While in line they can stare at my back if they want. Watch me cook. I'm both entertainment and chef. It's a proper day job for a collector. We have to have one—otherwise, people get suspicious.

"You look a little tired today, Radial."

I check two of the steaks and glance to my left. My manager, Korth, is standing there, smiling. He has dark skin and salted hair. He is also short, stout, and obnoxious. Never enough to be voted, I guess. He walks a fine line of annoyance. Plus, he's a manager, so he doubtless gets extra credit.

"Yeah, tired," I say, forcing a smile.

"Trouble sleeping?" he says. "And why is that? Too many shots? Too much playing? Too many women?"

I check the steaks again. Turn two, flip two. Built into the front of the grill is a rack for plates. I take a plate out and put the now-seared chicken on it. "Here," I say, handing him the plate.

He waves it away. "No way, can't help now. I'll get my shirt dirty. Got a meeting to go to."

"A meeting."

"Yeah, a big one. Might help decide my mother-in-law." He smiles and brings his hands together. "I've been waiting on that one a long time."

I shake my head, return my eyes to the grill. Part of what makes the system work is its anonymity. Korth is walking a line here too, talking about it.

He leans close. "You need to be happier, Mr. Crane. No one likes a sourpuss. Remember that. Votes accumulate."

As if he knows better than I. I look at him with narrowed eyes.

He seems to get my meaning. Waves a hand. "Not that I'd ever vote you, of course. You're important to me. Reliable."

I scowl.

He turns, lifts his hands to the crowd behind us, and raises his voice. "Welcome to the SmokeHouse, everyone! Who's ready for some fine dining? The juiciest steaks money can buy!" He lays a hand on my shoulder. "And Radial Crane here to prepare them for you. One of our best."

There is a scattering of cheers followed by halfhearted applause. I turn, smile, then take a bow, ever mindful of my green mushroom hat. The goal is to keep it in place. Our uniforms, yeah, solid green pants, striped green shirt. Skirts are an option for the gals. Mushroom hats for the guys. Caps for the girls.

Green is a popular color these days. It doesn't offend anyone.

Lanky brings me another order: two chicken breasts and a child's hot dog. In an alcove to my right is a stainless cooler where the meat is stored. It has two doors. The top door is for cheap meat and chicken. The bottom is for the primo stuff.

I need only the top door with this one. I free a spot on the grill—even use a little water to clean the space. Steam bursts into the air. I open the cooler and use tongs to put the chicken on. Best not to touch with the fingers, right?

I manage a glance at the line. Peeking above the counter is this dark-eyed boy. Waiting on the hot dog, I'd guess. His eyes are glued to what I'm doing. I force a smile and, reaching into the cooler, take out the dog and add it to my meat collection. The boy smiles. Hops a little. I glance at the couple who is with him. I assume they are his parents. Both have bright smiles on their face. Real or fake, I don't know. For his sake, I hope they're real. Hope they're good. They're lucky to have a child.

I return to my work. Steaks come off, steaks go on. Chicken, fish, sirloin. The grease drips, the smoke billows. People are happy and fed. Life is good.

An hour later, Jake comes in. He's my noon backup. He's a short guy, curly hair, a few years my junior. Always in motion. He smiles when he sees me. "Winning the war, Radial?"

I can't help but smile. "Taking prisoners." He has no idea. But he's the closest thing I have to a friend. I know he wouldn't vote me. Even if it mattered.

To the left of the grill is our fry station. It has a large deep-fat fryer and a rolling half-height freezer. The top of the freezer holds a tray and a warming light. That's where the prepared fried food is kept. To the left of all that is a huge two door oven—also stainless.

Those areas are now Jake's responsibility, along with helping me get items off the grill. The grill is cooking over a dozen items now, all in various stages of preparedness.

Grease flows like honey from a honeycomb. Smoke billows.

Jake makes a quick check of the fry station. Lifts the basket of cut potatoes, gives it a shake and re-immerses it in the fry grease. The frying resumes. He walks my direction, arms crossed. "You doing okay over here?" A glance at the grill. "Staying ahead?"

I nod. "For now," I say. "Thanks."

He turns to look at the grill. "I've got the boy tomorrow. Thinking about baseball. Want to come?"

"Night game?"

He nods. "At seven. Can you make it?"

I frown. Flip three steaks. Pull two off. Check the topmost order. "I'd like to," I say, "but I can't."

"Seriously, why not? It'll be fun! I always buy popcorn. Even for guests."

I smile. "Yeah, I'd like that." Above me is a long metal sliding track for the slips Lanky gives me. A way to track the orders. It is very low tech, very archaic. But that's part of this place's appeal. It is vintage. I slide the paper along. "But, you know…busy."

"Date?" Jake asks, hopeful.

I snort, shake my head. "Helping my aunt again," I say. "With her business." My aunt is a complete fabrication, as is the business. Unless you take it to mean Quantum. Then it works.

Jake looks genuinely disappointed, though that could be an act. Reality is hard to quantify these days. He gives my arm a slap. "I really wish you could come. Some other time, right?" He drifts toward his station again. "I mean it!"

"I know," I say. "You're a good guy, Jake."

He snorts. Puffs out his chest. "Yes, I am."

CHAPTER

It is seven-thirty. I'm at home, with the baseball game on vid. It is the third inning, and the Aquas are up four on the Rain. Nothing has been the same since the Seclusion, since everything went local. I miss the Mariners. National baseball.

My apartment is average size. A one bedroom with a parking space below the building. There is nothing either exemplary or disdainful about it. I sit on a burnt umber, fabric couch with my feet resting on a glass and wood coffee table. The apartment walls are off-white. Noncommittal. The vid is mounted on the wall across from me. It is 60" diagonal. Average size. To the right of the couch is a floor-standing tropical plant. Beyond that is a wide window with almond blinds. There's a plant near the window on the opposite wall as well.

I've consumed an average meal of a ham sandwich and bean soup. The remnants still sit on the table near my feet. Again, I'm waiting.

The Rain pitcher, Transom, is waiting too. He has the ball tucked behind his back. He stoops, checks the signal, and eases back. He checks first base, begins his motion.

Curve ball. Batter swings and misses. Strike one!

I smile and absently shove my plate back with a foot. On

the table next to the plate is one of the few pictures in my place. It is of me, Jake, and his young son Brian, at a game. It is nice because his son is between us with his arms around us both like we're family. Everyone is smiling. Brian is smiling largest of all. He has his cap on backwards and there's a dab of ketchup on his nose. Fun.

I check the game again. The batter swings at a fast ball. Another strike.

Collectors aren't supposed to have pictures, because they build connections. Jake would look for this picture if he ever came over, though. So I leave it out.

Plus, I like it.

A band of static appears at the top of my vidscreen, clears, and reappears. Then a second band appears at the bottom of the screen. The bands run in parallel for a full second, before disappearing completely. A pristine Transom prepares to throw, mitt to his face, eyes on the catcher.

Most would see the static as a glitch, a subtle failing of an otherwise perfect fidelity streamcast. But it isn't. Quantum knows my habits. How best to get my attention.

I walk to the bedroom. It is off-white with green carpet too. The walk-in closet is on the left. I open the closet door, work the switch that releases the false wall in back, and slide it open. There, neatly arranged on hangers, are my armored black suits. Above them, facing me on another shelf, are the masks. Five of them. Solid semblances of a human head—my head—all smoothed out and featureless. I pick a suit and a helmet, then spend the next ten minutes pulling them on. After the mask is in place I get a message that transportation is on the way. One perk of my job: curbside pickup.

Not at *my* curb, though.

My only hurdle is exiting my Queen Anne apartment undetected. That's not such a feat, since two of the apartment's four tenants are silicon junkies who work the wee hours of the night. The third is a bartender at an uptown concert venue. His workday began about two hours ago. I think I heard him leave, but to be sure…

I slide the hanging suits aside. Mounted on the wall behind

them is my surveillance panel. I'm able to tap camera feeds, get heat signatures, replay hours of audio. Right now it is configured to give me a topline summary. A simple tally of the building's occupants. That number shows only one person. Me.

The interior stairway is outside my door. After a last check of my suit—of my armaments and implements—I take my leave. I descend the stairs to the small lobby below. The exterior door is glass and well-lit. There is a camera trained on it, but as I walk by, it will momentarily glitch too. See only static. Another benefit of my suit: It wards off detection.

The sky is already dark. Outside the lobby is the visitor parking lot. I exit and walk to my left, past the edge of the building. There is an unlit alley between buildings that I slip into and follow. From there, it is easy to disappear into the streets.

No one questions a collector. Doing so is a good way to grease your vote total. Nobody wants that.

Ten minutes later, I'm at a nondescript crosswalk. A black van pulls up and stops. I get in. The inside is darkened, and there is a solid wall between the driver and me. I'm completely blocked off. I never see the driver. Nor do we talk. The only outside communication I get is from Quantum.

"Easy one tonight," Quantum says. "Non-criminal."

I don't say anything. Nothing is easy.

There are no windows in the van, but I've learned to detect some locations from sound alone. I can tell when we enter the highway, the shift and gentle curve as we exit. Then there's the *thump-thump-thump* of the northern bridge over the lake. We're headed to Eastside.

Twenty minutes later, the van stops.

"Surroundings?" I ask.

"Tech center," Quantum says. "Heavily lit. Your escort has selected a low light area. Expect little resistance."

The door opens to the parking lot of a three-story building. Clean, light-colored walls, lots of glass.

"First floor."

I nod to no one. The van quietly departs. Ahead and on the right, is the entrance to the building's subterranean parking garage. There is no gate. Between me and it there is only grass and lots of expensive landscaping. I crouch and move into the grass. I follow the building's shadow line, then enter the garage. It is lit in orange and doubtless has many cameras. Those will get the glitch treatment too, regardless of their level of sophistication.

It is past normal working hours, but there are plenty of cars in the garage. People working late. All makes and models, but mostly high performance sports cars, luxury cars, SUVs. I make my way to the middle of the garage and the glassenclosed entrance.

There is a sophisticated card reader here. A single swipe of my decoder and the door clicks free. I enter, pass by the elevators, and enter the stairwell. Best way to go unnoticed.

I ascend partway up and hear the door open above me. A twentyish man enters the stairwell. He is wearing a yellow shirt with a large black stripe on it. Around his neck is the latest net appliance, one that projects the visual onto whatever surface you hold in front of you. He's looking down as if in thought. Hurried. He takes three steps before he sees me. He startles, gasps, and places a hand to his chest. Finally, his eyes find the ground again, and he steps politely by me. "Sorry," he says.

He'll remember me for a few moments, then force himself to forget.

I reach the first floor. Four hallways radiate out from the stairway door. The carpet is forest green. The walls, off-white. No surprise. There is wire-frame art everywhere—both on the walls and floor-standing. Wire-frame in meaningless patterns. Meant to resemble nothing. Lots of green and off-white.

I feel a bit out of place. Workplace pickups are always weird.

Every hallway is filled with high-gloss wooden doors. One office after another. Numbered. There is little activity. It is well-lit but nearly empty. Few disturbances.

"One hundred and five," Quantum says.

"Got it." I check the signs on the corner. 105 is down the hall to my left. I head that direction, checking door numbers. About six offices in, a door opens on my right. Tall guy, fashionable lenses, button-down shirt. He's holding a notepad that he folds into him as I pass. He eases back into his office. I hear the door shut and lock behind him. I smile.

Two more offices then 105 is on my right. The door is closed, but the light is on inside. No need for the monitors here. I shrug and knock.

"Come in," a male voice says.

I rub the portion of my left glove that has the sniffer. Grip the door handle with it. I'm comforted when the back of the glove flashes blue. No explosives nearby. I didn't suspect there would be, but you never know with these tech-types. Make a mistake, and *blamo.*

I swing open the door. The office is neat, sophisticated. Doubtless a clone of every other office in the building. A large, wooden desk in the shape of an L, medium brown in color. Framed accomplishments hang on the wall. Posters of entertainment products. Celebrities.

The incon sits facing the corner. He has a circular vid there that he is engrossed in. Full dimension. Better than the screen I have at home. Images seem to hang in midair, perfectly formed.

I raise my right tranker. It would be better if he never turns.

He turns, though. He is Caucasian, dark hair, balding and a bit round. His face pales when he sees me. "Me? You've come for me? That can't be."

I shake my head. Better not to talk.

He pulls back in his seat, puts up both hands. "But why? How would I ever—?"

That's just it, it isn't *predictable.* Collection based on one wrong comment or behavior. It has little to do with right or wrong. Little to do with guilt. Only preference. Everyone else's preference.

Quantum feeds me data. I touch the switch that engages the mask's external speakers and put gravel in my voice. "You are Daniel Faust?"

"Yes, but I—"

"You have received incon status. Genetic verification will be done before full process."

"Full process? What does that mean? I just go away?"

I shake my head. "Ultimate disposition is not my concern," I say. "I only collect."

"But my wife! My children!"

"Were part of the process. They'll be updated."

His hands are still raised. He waves them nervously. "But can they survive? My house, my car—"

I frown inside the mask. The things people talk about. What does it say about us? About our society? I've heard that the eyes are the window to the soul, but I think that's wrong. It is speech. Has to be.

He rolls back his chair and abruptly stands. I don't much like that. Makes *me* nervous. "So what happens now?" he asks. "You lead me away like a common criminal? Like worthless trash?"

"If you like." I raise both arms so he can see the trank bracelets. "Or you'll be carried." I pause. "It's better if we don't make a scene. Less disturbing."

There's a flash of anger. "But I worked hard. I'm from a good family. A good neighborhood. I deserve—"

I shake my head. No more talking.

His eyes focus on the desk to his right. On the drawers. He begins to stoop.

"Touch nothing," I say.

He is shaking now. "I just want…" He looks at me. "You know, one for the road. Nothing wrong with that, is there?"

It would've been better if I'd blind tranked him. Tranks are resources, though. I'm not supposed to waste.

He's watching me, expectantly. He can't see my frown. "Slowly," I say.

He nods and pulls out the upper drawer. Retrieves a silver flask of something. Takes a swig. Looks at me. Then takes another. His eyes seem to redden. He sets the flask on the desk. "Okay," he says. "I'm coming."

I step into the hall and check for onlookers. See nobody. Wait for him to join me. I point in the direction of the stairwell. The elevator is near it, I know. He nods and walks up the hall ahead of me. We pass door after door. Finally, we reach the place where the hallways intersect.

He pauses. "How do you do this?" he asks. "How do you get picked?"

I've seen this game before. He wants the background chit-chat. Try to soften me. Get me to identify. I run through a sample in my mind.

I applied for security detail, Daniel. I was given a battery of tests. Some physical training. Then one day I came home to find a wrapped box in my apartment. My old apartment. Inside is a lock code to a particular vid channel. One that looks like fuzz to most people. With the code inserted, it clears up. Instructions are given. A life outside the vote. So I go for it. I've got nothing to lose. Plus, I know they chose me for a reason. That there was something about my makeup that made me a match. A prime collector.

"That is irrelevant," I say.

He stares at me. Nods acceptance. He indicates the elevator. I nod, and he pushes the down button. The door opens, and we step inside. The elevator is grey with golden highlights. Very distinguished for an elevator. There are mirrors on two walls. I push the button marked *P*.

I try not to look at him, but it is difficult.

He sniffles, then takes out a rag and wipes his eyes with it. "Allergies," he says.

Not allergies. Emotions. I avoid them whenever possible. Only complicates things.

There is a chime, and the elevator opens on the first floor. A young, dark-skinned man stands there, sheaf of papers in one hand. He looks at me and then at the incon. "Daniel?" he says, visibly surprised. "I have questions about the project. The benchmarks—"

I shake my head and press the *P* button again. The door closes, and we descend. We reach the parking garage and step out into the same secured room I entered from. I glance out the window. On the other side, idling, is a white van. The incon pats his back pocket. There's the lump of a wallet there. "You want to see pictures?" he asks.

I scowl. Bothering me, this one. Trying to make it hard. I open the exit door for him. Motion with my free hand.

He stalls, glares at me. "Is it too much for you to look at some pictures, Mask? Is that too much?"

The side of the van opens. The interior is the opposite of the van I arrived in. This one has plush carpeting, padded walls. Soft blues and pinks.

I place a hand on the incon's elbow, point toward the entrance. "Time to go."

He continues to stare at me. At my mask.

"You have full authority," Quantum says. "All options at your disposal."

I shake my head. I won't need more. I'm granite.

Finally, Daniel slumps his shoulders, and bowing, enters the van. "This is not fair, you know…"

But it is fair—fairer than God, they tell us. It is for the better. That's what I tell myself. That everyone's life is better as a result of what I do. Collecting. The incon starts to say something more, but I shut the door, closing him in.

The van pulls away into the night.

CHAPTER

I take my car to work the next day. I engage the autodrive and let it chauffeur me south toward the entrance to the Farmer's Market. As I approach, I glimpse the grey waters of the Sound to my right. To my left are a string of recently beautified apartments. All are precisely five stories tall and sparkling white.

I pass a building that used to house an art school. Art was always a risky proposition. Now it is riskier than ever. Usually it is done anonymously and with committees for input. That doesn't mean there isn't lots of art around, because there is. The city virtually dances with it. Only…nobody is taking credit.

I near the area where I typically park. A small lot just off First. I'm about to work the car's parking beacon—the device that tells the lot dealers that I'm looking—when a motorist parked street-side waves at me.

I check my mirror for traffic behind. All is clear, so I return to manual drive and stop.

The motorist, a forty-something lady, deftly angles her car out, freeing the space. I nod, smile, wave, and begin my own parking motion. The lady pulls up a bit and stops. She exits the car, smiling brightly. Waves.

I frown and wave again.

She approaches my window. She's dressed in a blue raincoat and carries an umbrella in one hand. Never a bad idea here.

I keep a miniaturized tranker under the seat for emergencies. I feel with my hand to make sure it is still there. I return her smile. Bring the window down.

She nods at the spot she vacated. "There's time left," she says. "Three hours, actually."

I pat my chest pocket where my wallet hides. "You want me to pay you?"

She waves off the offer. "No, please no. It's yours. Enjoy it."

I nod. "Thanks."

She reaches into her coat pocket and draws out a business card. "This is my card. Has my ident on it. I hope you'll remember me. Vote me."

I take the card, squint at it. Then at her. Average in appearance, a bit overweight. "Vote you?"

She shrugs. "Sure, you're nice, right? I think I'm low this month." She frowns and waves a hand near her face. "I've had some…things. Tough things."

I nod. Not much more I can do. "Strangers have less weight, you know. Barely register."

"Yes…" She waves again. "But it can't hurt, can it? Any little bit."

I shrug. "I suppose not."

She gives a closing wave and returns to her car.

I notice a slight hitch in her step. Injury or defect? I watch as she drives away. There's as much risk that I'd vote her down as up. Lobbying is frowned upon. But every behavior is suspect now. She was more blatant than most. Plus, if she has a defect…

I finish parking and open the door. I check the sky. Grey, like most other days. It isn't raining yet, though.

I secure the car and set off up Madison.

There are quite a few pedestrians out this morning. Most are dressed for the weather. A rainbow of slickers. Bright and cheery, despite the threat of rain. Everyone I pass smiles at me.

Greets me. Gives a gentle wave. I return them all, regardless of whether I have to or not. I have a role to play.

If they knew what I was, they might not be so friendly. Or maybe they'd be more so. I'm not sure.

Every behavior is suspect. Even the striking blond who waves at me now, showing teeth bright enough to tickle my stomach. Or her equally striking brunette companion.

It has been awhile, Radial. Companionship.

I raise the stakes on the blond, saying "Hi" as she draws closer. One eyebrow arches beautifully. Surprise, perhaps? She raises the stakes back at me, returning the salutation.

Now what are you going to do?

Same thing as I always do. I give a closing smile and continue on my way.

***

Ten minutes later, I'm in my uniform *greens* and walking up the steakhouse line.

Jake is already at the grill, steaks smoking, grease dripping, spats flipping. He smiles when he sees me. "Ready to feed 'em?"

I smile back. "Always." I check the order position to our right. Lanky isn't there. There's another girl, short and dark-haired. Marginally attractive. I think her name is Susan.

Substitution isn't that uncommon. Lanky's not the only order girl, after all.

"How was the game?" I ask. I know the Rain lost. Saw it on the news.

"Great!" Jake says. "Lost." A smile. "I'm sure you already knew that."

I shrug, smile. "Maybe…"

"Anyway, the kid loved it. Popcorn, you know."

I nod. I remember how it was. As a kid. It is muted, distant, but I remember the wonder. The hope.

I hear conversation on our right and look past Susan's counter to the hall beyond. A group of people are making their way in. Lunch rush beginning.

"Spuds good?" I ask.

Jake nods. "Got a couple dozen in the oven and one of the drawers full."

The stainless warming drawers hide beneath the counter behind me—the same counter orders are completed on. Two drawers for spuds, and one for rolls. A spud and a "voter approved" roll with every meal. Part of the deal.

I drift near the fry station. Give it a once over. There's a mound of fries under the light and a shrimp order, doubtless waiting for a steak to complete it. I glance at the red-tiled floor. Barely a sheen of grease there. The place is still clean. Jake was doing well.

Short Susan hands an order slip to Jake and brings another my direction. She crosses to the order completion counter and puts parsley on two otherwise ready plates. She slowly lifts the tray containing the order and follows the counter toward the dining room.

I check my slip. In SmokeHouse code it indicates a fried chicken sandwich. Beneath the fry station is a small two-shelf freezer. I open it and, reaching into the paper bag of chicken, bring out one of the frozen white triangles. Put it into the fry basket. Drop it. Watch as the fry grease consumes it. Makes it this bubbling white island amid a sea of brown.

"Excuse me, sir."

I turn toward the counter again. A dark-haired girl, probably nine years old, is there with a small plate in her hand. On it is a portion of ground chuck, clearly in the medium to medium-rare range.

I smile. "Yes?"

She notices my name tag. Focuses on the writing.

"It's Radial," I say.

She nods, looks at her plate. "Can you help me, Rad-i-al?" Her face scrunches, like she might be close to tears. "It has blood in it."

I scowl. "How did that happen?" I take the plate and walk to the grill. I keep an eye on the girl the entire way. Like I'm taking her with me. "Jake! Are you sleeping? This has blood! You know she doesn't want blood."

Jake looks at the girl. Raises a hand apologetically. "I'll fix it, milady. Right away." He returns the steak to the grill and starts to whistle a children's tune. Looks at her again and shrugs. "So sorry!"

I fake a kick at his behind, and the girl smiles. Returning to the counter, I lean close. "We'll bring it to you, okay?" I say. "This time, no blood."

She nods and smiles. Goes on her way.

I drift Jake's direction. He has about a half a grill of steaks. Manageable. No help needed.

He motions with his head and I draw closer still. "I think Lanky got voted," he whispers.

"Why do you think that?" We're not supposed to care. A person ruled an incon? Such a person shouldn't be missed.

He flips a burger. Gives it a closing pat with his spats. "Didn't show this morning."

"She was on order detail?"

Jake shakes his head. "No. Register. Korth is there now." A pause. "Still…didn't show."

The register is at the end of the line. I rarely follow the line to its conclusion. My place is here. With the heat and grease. "Maybe Lanky is running late too," I say. "Emergency."

"Maybe," he says, "but I don't think so." He turns three steaks, moving them left in the process. He selects a ground chuck and folds it. Exposes the inside. Still pink. "Do you think it is right?" he says.

I frown. "The steak?"

He shakes his head. "No, the process. The voting."

I feel a lump in my throat. No one gets voted for dissent. That's not how it works. Free expression is still allowed. Still lauded. But you shouldn't offend too many. Some people *love* the system. Love the blind competition. The rush.

I shrug. "It is the way it is. The population—"

"If we believe what they say." He checks the tickets overhead. "How would anyone know? Do they still count?"

They did until ten billion. Then they made a decision. Every nation in its own way, but they all contribute. Our sector, PacNorth, has its own problems. Seclusion. Necessities. Survival.

Jake brings out a plate and slides a steak on it. Removes the appropriate order ticket and hurries them both to the prep station.

"I rarely think about it." Which is true. I'm not paid to think. Only to act.

He examines his orders again. "Yeah, most don't. As long as it isn't them that's 'inconvenient.'"

I stare at the grill. Two sirloins are bubbling red on top. In need of flipping. "Incon," I say. "They're called incons."

Jake chuckles. "Same meaning."

I drift toward my station again. The chicken is fully floating now. Nearly done. Atop the warming light is a pair of metal tongs. I reach for them.

Holding two steak-filled plates, Jake moves near me. "Now we live with the cloud overhead. The masks in the night."

The other goal of the system was to motivate people to greatness, to likability. *Too much vitriol,* they said. So the whole thing, everything and everyone, became votable. A possible thumbs up or down. That was the decision. The necessity.

I don't want this discussion, but sometimes you have to play human. Jake is a good guy. Seemingly.

"They must be cold," he says. "Those masks." He points a plate at my station. "Like a frozen chicken. Solid, hard, and cold."

He swings back toward the counter. I hear his plates rattle as they make contact. Orders ready for completion. He comes my way again. Smiling. "Pass two at the order counter."

Pass two is code, meaning there's an attractive female nearby. I stare at the bubbling fry grease a few moments more. Don't want to be obvious. When it is clear the chicken is done—brown—I retrieve a plate and pluck it from the grease. Set it politely to one side of the plate, and turn to take it to the counter. My chance.

I scan the line of slowly advancing faces. I glance right, center, and finally left to where I know the "pass two" should be. I startle, not only because the girl *is* strikingly pretty, but because I've seen her before. The blonde from earlier.

I glance at my greens. Great way to make an impression.

I move to the counter and place the chicken on the waiting prep tray. I can't help but look the girl's direction, though. This time, her eyes find me. She stares for a moment, then smiles. Her hand, resting on the counter in front of her, gives a little wave.

I feel heat in my chest and face. Thankfully, I have lots of reasons for that in the kitchen. I manage to smile back and lift my right arm. Shrug at my situation. Return to my work.

Bah.

Jake faces the grill, but he's smiling. Possibly chuckling.

I can feel the blonde's gaze on my back. Absolutely real. Present. Waiting?

Nothing I can do. I'm working. I check the wall-mounted potato timer. Five minutes until the next pull. Too much time.

Jake brings a plate out of his rack. Clanks it on the stainless grill front, plates a steak—a filet, I think—and tears the appropriate order slip down from above. He moves to the prep area. Short Susan brings me another order. I stare at it but don't really see it.

Should I say something?

I am the mask. The mask is me.

I scowl, focus on the new order. Another chicken.

I can hear Jake talking to someone in the line, but I'm hesitant to look. To gawk. Pretty girl! I open the small cooler, reach for the chicken bag.

Jake approaches, order slip in hand. I glance at him, feel inside the bag for the chicken. My hand finds an icy morsel. Pulls it out. Jake lays the order slip on the sliver of fry station counter, face down. Written in bold blue is a number. He smiles. "Her ident. She says to call her."

My mouth opens on its own. I clamp it shut and look over my shoulder. The blonde is almost directly behind me now. I turn and she smiles. I wave and pick up the order slip. Smile. Make a show of putting it in my front pocket. "Thanks," I say.

Jake stares at me. "So, do you know her?"

"I..." I drop the chicken into the basket. Release it to the grease. "I met her on my way in."

"Vote fishing?" he asks.

Like the lady with the limp? The one who gave me her parking spot? I frown. At least that one was honest. But this one? That smile? "Maybe," I say. "But I hope not."

Jake slaps me on the shoulder. "Me too. Because you need a life." He smiles, returns to his station.

Complications. As much as I try to avoid them, they keep asserting themselves.

But I am the mask.

CHAPTER

Two nights later.

Following another job, my fourth of the night, Quantum releases me. I'm returned to my apartment building, where I creep soundlessly inside. Once back in my room, I remove the mask and return it to its shelf in the hidden closet. Next comes the various gadgets I carry—the tranks and monitors—all carefully re-shelved. Then the suit. Flexible, yet rugged. Sturdy. I take it off and examine the entire surface, looking for breaks, chips, or cuts. I find nothing substantial.

At the bottom of the closet is an oval-shaped cleaning device. It has no name, since it is specially made for the suits of my trade. Consumer garment cleaners don't even approach its sophistication. I snap open the top half of the oval, weave the suit through the machine's cleaning chamber, then close the top and push the button to activate. The machine will anneal any micro-tears, fumigate, sterilize, and steam clean. The suit will be good as new. Ready for another night.

I reseal the closet door and pull out clothing for myself—casual wear—and head for the shower.

Ten minutes later, I'm dressed and clean. Radial reborn. I walk into the living area, pass the couch and coffee table to the window, and look out.

The street beyond the complex is sleepy this time of night. The only illumination is from the streetlights. The only action? The drizzle of rain. I would leave this city if I could. Get away from the rain.

Such relocation is impossible now. Voted on and ratified by the majority. The broken union has fewer habitable areas than it used to, each forming its own authority. Its own seclusion. Balance must be maintained.

It *is* for the best. I believe that.

There are natural forces that hem in the sector too. A chain of smoke and fire just outside the picturesque scenery. Cross-sector air travel is not only illegal now, it is dangerous.

That's why Jake's ruminations are false. The process is necessary. Necessary and fair. A vote weighted in favor of those who know you? What could be fairer than that?

If they don't want you enough to keep you around…well, you aren't trying.

I remember the girl's contact information. I get a twinge of worry that I might have lost it, then another twinge that I haven't. It's been two days!

I jog to the bedroom and search the floor for the uniform. Not finding it there, I walk to the brown wicker hamper by the wall. It is filled with uniforms. I begin tossing out green-striped shirts and solid pants. Mostly I focus on the shirts, testing them to find a place that suggests paper. I go through the whole hamper but find nothing.

Frowning, I look at the pile on the floor. I stoop and begin sorting shirt from pants. Two piles. Respectable and polite. Efficient. I take the shirt pile one by one. Hold them up, shake them out, test the front pocket. Three shirts in, I'm rewarded by the feel of something in the pocket. I smile and fish the order sheet out. Study it. Wonder if it is legit.

If someone in a green uniform, with a mushroom hat, asked for your number for a friend, would you give it?

Can't say I would.

So did she? Really?

I wander back to the living area, sheet in hand. I sit at the couch and grab the vid controller. The controller is an amorphous grey sack, really. It is able to conform to your hand, reading the movements of fingers and palm. It is fully configurable and haptic in both directions. Useful, but also a bit disturbing. A lot like squeezing a rat.

First contact with someone is typically voice only. Text, if you want to be extra cautious. Image comes later. My screen supports all three, simultaneously or separate. Delivered directly and discretely. Top of the line.

Another advantage of the vote—for those who remain convenient, *top of the line* is always available.

I turn the vid on and check the time. It is late. Much too late for direct contact by vid or speech. After two in the morning!

Story of my life. Quantum comes first, even when she doesn't have to.

So, should I do anything? Send the young lady a note?

It has been two days. I am the mask.

A late-night note should be acceptable. I contemplate what to say, how to phrase it. Everyone is bubbly these days. I try to compose myself for upbeat and bubbly. I realize I can't manage that with image. Speech is marginal. Text is too impersonal.

I shake my head. What am I doing?

I think a little longer.

Finally, I shrug. I'm supposed to fit in. Supposed to be normal. Talking to females is normal. I configure the screen for speech and begin talking. I stop and restart four times before I'm satisfied. I even adjust the wave pattern to make sure I'm bubbly enough and interesting enough. I send the message away. Hopefully she's still interested. Doesn't wonder why I'm sending speech so late at night.

She'll probably think I'm an insomniac. Which is okay. Many people are. Despite appearances, it is hard to hide from the system. The vote. Most are medicated at night. Sleep on demand.

Not me. I always sleep just fine.

I'm part of the system.

CHAPTER

I'm awakened by the chiming sound of my living room vid. Odd, because I normally have the chime off. There are only a handful of people I'll let the thing wake me for. A very small list. Most of them are work-related contacts. My *day* work, of course. At the SmokeHouse.

I climb my way out of bed, pull on an old shirt and sweats, and stumble toward the living area. A light on the vid top is flashing. The screen itself is still black. Waiting for me to wake it.

I glance at the windows and see that there's been a break in the rain. Sunlight is pushing through. It is as bright as I've ever seen it, in fact—the parking area is a lighter, dryer, shade of grey.

I drop into the couch and work the vid control pad. The screen brightens, shows a rippling sunburst pattern with the manufacturer name, then dissolves into a page showing Jake's still image. His mouth is partly open and he's looking to his right. His expression appears troubled. Something has happened.

I work the "converse" button on the control. Jake's lips begin to move. His eyes are still looking right, not at his screen—so, not at me. I notice a trace of redness. He is upset. Or really tired.

"I can't believe it. Don't know why she'd…"

I straighten in my seat. Lean forward. "Jake!" I say. "What is it?"

He looks me in the face. His eyes *are* red. Emotional.

"Amy, Radial. She's gone. Taken my boy."

Jake split with Amy some time ago. Splits don't happen as much as they used to. Usually one or the other of the partners gets voted before that happens. Usually the one with the larger and most tight-knit support group *wins*, if you can call it that.

Kids are placed with someone, regardless. Someone low on votes. They are placed with the parents to begin with, after all. No one carries to term anymore. Too inconvenient. Children are on demand too.

"You don't think she—?"

"Got voted?" Jake shakes his head. "No. I'd be the one to get the kid anyway, right? He'd come to me."

It is possible that *both* got voted. I don't mention that to Jake.

"It is killing me, Radial. I can't lose him too."

"Meds," I say. "You have some? Script up to date? Because I can—"

Jake looks hard at me. Even through the ether, his eyes are screaming. "Don't talk to me about meds, man. This is real. Freaking system. Hate those masks. Freaking vote."

I shake my head. "You said she didn't get voted."

"I don't know, Rad. Don't know anything anymore. I just know they're gone."

Usually I distance myself from the missing. It is difficult this time, though. I've met Jake's son. I *know* Brian. I know what he looks like. What he likes to eat. I notice the picture on the coffee table. Brian's arm over my shoulder. Kids.

Jake is quiet for a time, again looking to his right. "Does it seem like there are more now?" he asks then.

"More voted away?" I shrug. "Don't know." My collection rate has stayed pretty even. There could be more masks now, though. Those numbers are secret. They have to be. Only Quantum knows.

Jake's head is down, as if searching the floor. "What am I going to do?"

"Did you sleep?" I ask.

He shakes his head. "Not really, no." He glances at me. "I just found out last night."

I nod. Sympathetically, I think. "You should sleep. That will help. You let the authorities know, right? So wait it out."

He coughs sarcastically. "Wait for what? A message telling me they're gone?" A tear escapes his left eye. "How could they have been collected? I didn't vote either of them."

"You don't need to tell me that," I say. "Votes are private."

His eyes go hard again. "But I want you to know. I didn't. I wouldn't." A pause. "Like I'd never vote you."

I nod. "Okay…" This has happened before, this uncomfortable situation. Not as many times as to most people, probably. I don't know. But it is something I have to shield against. "You should get some rest," I say. "Maybe take something—"

"I have lunch today," he says.

I resist looking at the window, the sunshine. "I can do it," I say. "I'll work for you."

He shakes his head. "No. I need the credits. Got bills." A stifled sob. "Still haven't paid for those baseball tickets."

Over Jake's image I bring up a text overlay of the current time. It is still early. "Well, get some rest then. You have a few hours. Can't do anything unless you've slept."

Jake gives a reluctant nod. Looks at the floor again. "Yeah…right. Okay." He manages a little wave. "I'll rest like you say…"

The screen goes black.

I sit for a moment, thinking. It is unusual for two people to be taken at once, but not unheard of. Plus, if one resists for another, it's a quick way to get a full vote against. Save the mask a trip. Like the girlfriend from a few nights back. The one who decided to attack me. When it is your time, it is your time. That's the process.

The number of negative votes that are required varies based on age. In its original form, the formula was simple: Every decade of life adds another vote necessary to rule you an incon. At birth, you require only two. Pre-born…well, they only ever required one negative, right? Ten year olds require three. Twenty year olds require four. Thirty year olds, five…etc.

The formula got more complicated when they added pro-votes. There is an offsetting factor with those. The weight is heavier the more closely associated the person is to the voter.

The vote is tallied on your birthday each year. Doesn't mean you're collected that day. Could be weeks later. Months. It also means people tend to be nicer around their birthdays. Occasionally you see lobbying. But not much. Lobby too much, and people start neg-ging you just because.

It is a balancing act, but that's life. A high-wire act that nobody ultimately survives.

I think about Jake again. Look out the window at the sunny day. Shrug. Maybe I'll go to the zoo.

My screen chirps at me. Jake again?

A message box pops up. The image is clearly not Jake. It is the blonde. Even frozen in place, she looks completely composed. Perfect straight hair, blue eyes, shining white teeth. Beautiful. I glance at the rumpled clothing I have on. There are small stains on my shirt. A tear at the knees of my sweats. No way can I take this call now.

The box flashes at me, waiting. Actively waiting.

Do I ignore and get back to her later? Or risk looking like a lump?

The top right of the screen features a gear-shaped option icon. I work that and set active video off. Nothing impolite about morning shyness, right?

Her image adjusts slightly. Now I can see that her eyes have moved, as if she's checking the corner of her screen. Noting the change I've made. I work the converse button. Her image begins to move. I note her name on the screen: Heather Black.

She smiles. Her eyes look first my direction, then back at the corner of her screen. "Hiding out this morning, huh?"

I smile without her knowing. "Not a morning person," I say. "Sorry."

"Maybe I shouldn't be either. I'm sure I look terrible."

I study her image. I've seen highway vidboard models that look worse. "You look amazing," I say. "Great!"

She rolls her eyes. "Flatterer" She pauses. "So you're a cook?"

I chuckle. Right to the profession. Not unusual in today's world. "With a limited recipe list. But, yeah, steak and potatoes, I can do."

She laughs. "You'd be surprised how many can't. That's a skill!"

Friendly. Nice. Might be near her birthday.

"Are you sure you can't turn your vid on?" she asks. "Feels like I'm talking to a wall."

I shake my head. For some reason. "Seriously, I just got up. You don't want to see me."

"Are you clothed?"

"...yes..."

A brighter smile. "So, no problem. Show yourself!"

Another pointless head shake. "No. Can't. Sorry."

"I have a birthmark." She holds her arm up where I can see it. Pulls a white sleeve down. On the otherwise flawless skin is a small diamond of brown. Still perfect. Only brown perfect. "There. Do you see it?" she asks, pointing.

I snort. "Yes. It is hideous."

She laughs. "So now you can show yourself. I've shown you my worst feature."

"Wow..." I'm either on the verge of being annoyed or wildly attracted. Given that I'm smiling, probably the latter. I just wish I knew if she was real. That's the problem. What is real?

I stand and jog to the mirror that hangs behind my front door—a habit I learned from my father. Always check yourself on the way out.

My hair is naturally curly, so a night of sleep has done little to alter it. The largest stain on my shirt is near the bottom. I can adjust the vid to cut that out. Actually, if I were more familiar with the screen's features, I could probably digitally alter the shirt altogether. Or I could simply change my shirt.

Whatever. I'll pass.

"You still there, Radial?"

"Yes, yes…" I return to the couch and squint at the screen options again. I run a test grab of my image and zoom it over Heather's still moving face. Make sure it looks okay. That the stains are out of the picture. I then close the test window. Heather's face is still there. Smiling. I add vid to my side of the conversation. Now Heather's smile gets even brighter. A good sign.

"There you are!" she says. "See, now I know I'm talking to the right person. None of that shy lurker stuff."

I smile. "I wasn't lurking." I feel shy now, though. Like I want to stare a hole in the coffee table. Or the floor. But I can't. I know that. Got to keep looking up. At her eyes. Stay polite. Proper. "What do you do?" Back on profession. That's proper, right?

She tells me she has something to do with the robot harvesters that work the crops in the valley to the east. Programs them. Or manages them. Something. After the first sentence, it was over my head. I use tech, but I know little about how it works. Might as well be magic. Thankfully, my magic can take a lot of abuse.

Her magic is more important, though. I know that. The farms are what feed PacNorth. Otherwise, we'd all be dead. "Sounds interesting," I say.

She laughs. "Your eyes glazed over. That what you mean by interesting?"

I blush. "Guilty."

Her smile dwindles, then her face takes on a reflective look. "You're unique, Radial."

I shake my head. "I'm not, really. Just average. Typical."

"Hmm… I have to go soon. Work."

I nod. "Right. Of course. You should. Right."

Another hint of a smile. "So, you messaged me."

"Right. I did." I force my eyes up again. Why do they seek the tabletop? Why do I feel like I have no control? "Want to get together later? Maybe lunch…or the zoo?"

She is quiet for a moment, studying me. "I can do lunch at the zoo. Sure. Not far from one of our offices, actually."

I manage a smile. "Good. Great, actually."

"Glad you think so." She chuckles again.

We negotiate the detail. Meet by the entrance. Noon sharp. Lunch in hand. I'll pay for the zoo only. That works.

I think how good it is that I showed myself. That way, she'll recognize me. Then I realize she's seen me before anyway. Twice. That she's not me. That, for her, faces and personalities don't blur into obsolescence after only a few hours' time. That she might even care about something.

We say our goodbyes. She has work.

I don't. Not today. Not tonight.

And I'm okay with that. I have the zoo.

CHAPTER

Lunch at the zoo is good. Normal. We meet at the entrance as planned. It is still sunny. We walk the entire circle of the Australia and Asia exhibit—complete with aged wallabies and a lonely snow leopard—before finding a place to sit near the orangutan pen.

She tells me of her family, two parents and a brother, and their employment. She says how lucky they are. How votes have been kind to them. Not that she doesn't consider the vote itself kind, only that it is nice to win. To continue as you are.

That is a common belief.

She asks about my family. I keep things general. I don't tell her I lost an older brother to the vote. Only that my mother and father are still alive but separated. Physically about as far apart as they can be in this strange sector we call home.

All the while my mind wanders to Jake. His feelings. His missing son and ex-wife. If only he'd medicate. Then he'd feel fine, right? Better.

Heather and I make our way first to the giraffes and then the lions. The whole zoo is designed to look as habitat-native as possible. If anyone really remembers what that was. For the lions, that means lots of tall grass and large shade trees, apparently.

There is one male lion, seated on the ground beneath a large oak. He raises his head when we approach, like we are the first humans he's seen all day. Regardless of the fact that there is a trickle of people ahead of us. Somehow, he notices us. He stares long and hard before finally resting his head again on his feet. Behind him, partially obscured by the tree, is an ever-pacing female. Her eyes have been watching everyone from kid to grownup. Both animals look worn out to me. Stuck.

Heather rests her arms on the decorative metal fence that separates us from the cats. Beyond that is a small gully, seemingly too small to keep full-grown lions in. But it is probably safe.

"The females do all the hunting," Heather says.

I look at her, but she's still studying the animals, eyes squinted. "What?"

Now she turns to me. Smiles. "Yeah, the females do all the work. The male just sits around and waits." She raises a finger. "Usually under a tree. Just like that one."

I shrug. "A good life then."

She makes teasing contact with my shoulder. "For him. Yeah. Sure."

I was talking about the females. But Heather doesn't need to know that, does she? Maybe. I shrug again. "I meant her. Good to be active. To be *doing* something."

Heather stares at the ground. Moves a pebble with her foot. "I suppose that's true. Active, right? That's what we all are." She reaches out and takes my hand. "You're okay, Radial Crane."

We move away from the lions. Drift to the sinewy ocelots, and then to the gorillas. These have a small crowd in front of them. The pen front is transparent, with a dirt and grass floor beyond. There is a large central tree with suspended ropes and swings. There are climbing rocks around the perimeter.

I stand on tiptoe to see over the tight crowd. A large male is front and center, and he is clearly aware of the audience. His eyes search the length of collected humans as if he's about to speak. Then he collects a mound of feces from the ground next to him. Holds it. Studies it.

And eats it.

Children shriek. Parents groan.

"Ew," Heather says. "Let's not stay here."

I suppress a chuckle. Move on with her. There is a decorative carousel directly ahead. Plastic animals forever spinning. Brash versions of children's melodies playing clanky and loud.

Heather brings her hand up, taking mine with it. Checks her watch. "I need to go," she says. "Back to work." A frown. "Sorry. I can take an hour and a half occasionally. But two is pushing it."

"That's all right."

We make our way to the zoo exit. When we reach it, she turns to me and takes both hands in hers. "Thanks so much for today. It was wonderful."

I nod. Squeeze her hands in reply.

"I'm glad your friend got my number." She smiles brightly. Teasingly.

It only reminds me of Jake, though I force a smile. "Sometimes I need help."

I never need help. Never want it. I am the mask.

"Well, I'm glad he helped you then." She leans forward and kisses my cheek. She waves, and walks away.

CHAPTER

I spend a few more hours at the zoo after Heather leaves. Not really stopping anywhere. Just walking. Passing animal enclosures. Elephants and bears, lions and tapirs. Some notice me. Most don't.

The only animals that spend more than a passing moment on me are those in the raptor pen. Here a black cage forms the entire enclosure. Three falcons appraise me as I slow to look at them. One even drops from his high wooden perch to the floor and hops my direction. His head turns first to favor one eye and then the other. Heavy study.

A raptor. Watching *me*.

Funny.

Back at home, I find my normal place on the couch. I wake the vid and check messages. Nothing but junk. Offers to make a foreign million, products to improve my appearance—even one to join a "sting posse," whatever that means.

VoteMAX asserts itself. It has been awhile since I've voted and it has missed me. Needs my input.

I grab the controller sack and give it a strong squeeze,

enough that I know it has checked my identity five ways. It responds with a pulse of light and a burst of warmth. Plus, it gives a slight twitch. Personally, I don't much like the twitch. Disturbing. Like a rat!

It presents a list, complete with pictures, of every person I've had the likelihood of interacting with during the week. Next to each is a simple binary choice of "Yes" and "No." The voting matrix. Locations are tracked and cross-tabulated. Weighted for time in close proximity. Many of the faces are strangers to me. Incidental contacts from the SmokeHouse, probably. Those I've spent the most contact with are near the top of the list.

Heather is number one. I quickly select "Yes" for her, then skim through the rest of the list. I always "Yes" Jake, because I know he is yessing me. I notice the woman who gave me her parking spot. Even though it was a clear quest for votes, I yes her too. She was helpful.

I push VoteMAX away, and I think of Jake. Wonder if he made it to work. I message him at home. I let the screen check for over a minute. No answer.

I'm not supposed to care. The less I get involved, the better. But I'm curious. Masks are supposed to be curious, right? I think about calling work, but that would mean talking to Korth or one of his mindless assistants. Plus getting chastised for calling at work.

I frown and page through the screen's entertainment options. Pause on a baseball game. Not the locals this time. Some historical Mariners contest.

I last only ten minutes with that before I have to stand. Have to do something. Need action.

▲▲▲

Twenty minutes later, I'm at the SmokeHouse. It is well past lunch but not quite dinnertime, so the parking lot is nearly empty. The SmokeHouse building is circular and light brown with a red coned roof. Windows line the exterior, and there's a portico that juts out to indicate the front. Only uniformed employees are allowed through the rear door, so I head for the portico.

Inside, the decoration is bland cowboy. Wood paneling from about waist level down, patterned cow and bull wallpaper above. There's a serpentine rope corral for customers to move through—currently empty—so I duck under it until I reach the order counter.

Short Susan is there again. No Lanky. Dark hair peeks out from beneath Susan's cap. A large strand falls into her face. She blows it out of the way as I reach her. "Hey, Radial," she says, smiling. "What do you need?"

There's a wall that blocks my direct view of the grill, so I lean to the left and look around her. The grill has about three items on it. All burgers. Minding the grill, spats in hand, is Korth. "Jake's not here?" I say.

Susan glances at the grill. "Yeah, he called in. Says he's sick." She frowns, lowers her voice. "Korth is scorched. Big bad mood."

I nod. "No surprise."

If Jake is home he isn't answering his vid. Sleeping? Maybe. Hopefully he didn't hurt himself. Hopefully he's okay.

"Probably shouldn't let him see you if you don't want to work," Susan says.

Part of me wants to work. Distract my mind. The other part feels tired. Even with the sunshine outside.

I get this gnawing feeling I should check on Jake. That he might need my help. Then I wonder if there is a way for me to contact Quantum. She would know, right? She could tell me if Jake's people *were* voted. If they were taken away.

I am granite. I'm not supposed to care. This was the method that was decided to control growth. To keep it static.

After the eruptions. After the breakup, the Seclusion. When PacNorth became a state unto itself. We're maintaining as best we can. With what we have. Surviving.

In the system. All part of the system.

Korth walks around the corner, spats in hand. "Radial Crane!"

"Sir…"

He clangs the spats together like I do when I'm nervous. Except his *clang* is more forceful. "You want to work today?"

I shake my head. "No. Can't." I have to check on Jake. I step back and feel the rope line grab the back of my legs.

"I really need your help," Korth says. "Jake had part of dinner rush too." I notice Korth has a grease stain on his tie. He must hate that. "Seriously. I need you."

Most workers would care. Would *need* to care. But I don't. Not really. "Day off." I duck under the first rope line then step close to the second.

"Come on, Radial! I'll make it worth your while. Give you any day off next week. Free meal vouchers!" He raises the spats. Smiles. "And votes! I can get you votes." He looks at Susan. "You'd vote for Radial, wouldn't you?"

Out of line, that last comment. His first offer has value, though. Being able to choose my day, even on the weekend, is big. Especially if there's a possibility of another date with Heather. Which I think there is if that gorilla incident didn't leave a bad taste in her mouth. So to speak.

I frown, shake my head. "I don't have a uniform," I say. "Sorry."

"We have others in the back." Korth looks serious. "What's your size?"

Like a dog with a bone. Doesn't give up.

I *did* tell Jake I'd cover for him. "Will you go easy on Jake?" I ask.

That seems to surprise Korth. "What do you mean?"

"You know. I don't want you badmouthing him. Or negging him. Telling other people to. He's having it hard right now."

Korth spreads his hands. "Hey, I'm not like that, Radial."

I frown. "No?"

"No, man. I like Jake. He's a good worker." A smile. "Wish he were here now!"

"Right. Me too."

Korth's hands lower. Smile brightens. Behind me, I hear the portico door open. A family of customers enter. "So will you help me? I mean it, whatever day you want off. Free food."

I glance at the tiled floor. Jake, man, are you all right? "Until when?" I ask.

The customers reach me in the line. A fortyish couple with two teens in tow. They pause. Look confused. I back up so they can step by. The lady smiles and passes me. Her arms are crossed over her yellow rain slicker.

"Only until six. I'll find someone else for dinner. Just give me the rest of the afternoon."

"Fine."

I wind my way back through the rope and then outside. Head for the rear door.

CHAPTER

It is almost seven before I leave. Two tour busses arrived at six, filled with geriatrics. End of life tours are more popular now than ever, and the SmokeHouse is a common stop.

I've heard that the elderly used to finish their life in government care facilities surrounded by their peers. I've never seen such a facility, though. I doubt they ever existed. They certainly aren't necessary now. Taking the resources of others is by definition inconvenient. And nobody wants that.

Regardless, old tourists still know how to eat. My grill was filled to capacity for most of an hour. My replacement, Rob, got in at six like Korth promised. But there was no way I could leave with a full grill. He's too new at this.

His mushroom hat almost stood at attention when he saw what I was up against. "Please tell me you're not leaving."

So I stayed. Helped.

Now I'm on my way to Jake's. Just to check. That would be normal, right? Humane.

Jake lives in a small rambler a few miles north of my place. Driving, I ascend Queen Anne hill and gawk at the pedestrians. There are many out, despite the pending darkness. Groups of shoppers and couples walking. Beautiful people, really. Each with lots of friends, undoubtedly. Lots of possessions.

I reach the stop sign at the apex of the hill—a nightmare when snow comes, but nice this evening. There are restaurants on all sides of me. All good ones. With lots of favor. Lots of votes.

I drive two more streets and turn right down Boston, then down one of the numbered streets. Finally, I arrive outside of Jake's. Daylight is waning now, but his house is close enough to the corner streetlight that I can see fairly well. It is a typical old-style cedar-sided home, colored sepia—another popular non-offensive color. The roof is grey and appears to be cedar too. Except I know it isn't. Cedar shakes got voted long ago. Too dangerous. Too destructive. Too wasteful. Now only manufactured materials are allowed.

I park on the street and walk to the door. It is medium green with a brass handle. Nice. The locks are archaic. Easily thwarted. That shouldn't be necessary now, though.

I ring the doorbell. Wait. Expect to hear movement or the sound of the lock unlocking. Even the archaic ones are typically remote-controllable. But after several moments, there is still silence.

To the right of the door is a window. I lean over peer through to the inside. There are window blinds in place. I can see darkened objects, hints of furniture, but no more. I frown. Try knocking. Still no response.

Now what? I knock again and call out Jake's name. I wait. Wonder. Feel a bit unsettled for not having come earlier. Maybe he's away? Baseball game, even?

He hasn't paid off the tickets from earlier game, though. Can't imagine him going again so soon. Not without his son.

I look at my car. That nondescript Chevler 505. "A man's sedan," they call it. What it is, in fact, is just enough innovation and curves to keep people happy. Safe, incremental change.

Along with my miniature tranker, I keep a low grade decoder there. It wouldn't have freed the locks of the tech building from a few nights ago, but it'll do Jake's lock just fine.

Except if someone finds out I have one, and used it, my cover is completely blown. And that's not good. Losing my cover is a cardinal sin.

I drift toward the car, checking the street as I go. The nearest houses are quiet. Lights on inside, but otherwise no action. I can hear a dog's sporadic bark from a couple of houses over and smell the hint of pine. There's an occasional shout with laughter from somewhere. Probably the area with the restaurants.

I reach the car door, open it, crouch, and take my small decoder from beneath the seat. This one is oval too, but it fits neatly in the palm of my hand. Passersby wouldn't even notice I was holding it. I quietly shut the door and return to Jake's front porch. I try the doorbell one last time. Then with a final look both directions, I decode the door. I smile when I hear it click open. I glance behind me and quickly step inside.

I get a bad feeling, a weight that wasn't present all the other times I've been here. A big heavy. I should've called the authorities. Let soft enforcement check it out. What would I say, though? That my coworker didn't show up for work? What attention would that get?

Jake could be hurt. He's all alone now, so no one would've summoned help.

I call his name again. I know, at least, that one of my brethren hasn't gotten to him. Collections happen only at night, but it isn't dark enough. Late enough.

I scan the living room. There are no lights on. The only interior illumination comes from a fish tank on the wall opposite the front door. It is a fairly large tank, so that helps. I make sure the front door is shut and palm the wall light switch. "Jake…man… It's Radial…"

To my right, along the wall, is a short, olive desk, complete with a matching chair. The wall to my left sports a fireplace with Jake's darkened vid hanging above it. Straight ahead is a couch long enough to stretch out on without touching your feet at the end. It is beige with hints of that same olive color. There's a medium brown coffee table in front of the couch. On it is Jake's reading tablet, also darkened. Next to that is the biodegradable wrapper from a local sandwich shop. Italian, I think. Nothing you could buy at the SmokeHouse, anyway. Real loyal, that Jake.

Past the living room is a small dining area and the kitchen. Nothing appears out of the ordinary there. The bedrooms are ahead on my right. I move past the couch, briefly gazing at the sandwich wrapper again. "Tallies" it says, along with the picture of an underweight female figure. Nearly starving.

Frowning, I step into the adjoining hallway. There are two bedrooms. There isn't much light here. I feel uncomfortable again. Like I'm intruding. Infecting some place I shouldn't be. Weird feeling for a mask. Plus, I know Jake. I've been in this hallway before. Yet I feel naked without my suit now. My gear.

"Jake…?"

The nearest bedroom is on my right. Jake's. If he is sick, incapacitated, this is where he should be. The door is partially open. I take a few steps and lean forward so I can see. In the far corner of his room Jake has a bio-light. Tendrils of glass swirl up and around each other and finally meet in a peak at about a meter high. Inside are living bioluminescents. Keep them watered and well fed, and you have low cost lighting. This particular light is from when the fad was new. It puts an eerie purple pallor over the entire room. The end of Jake's bed is visible. It looks smoothed out. Still made. I give the door a small push. It swings freely.

The room is empty.

I snort. Wonder what to do next. I advance to the spare room. The one typically used by Jake's son. The door here is closed. I reach for the handle and ease it open. The room is in total darkness, but I think I hear something. A dry rasp. I reach for the wall where the light switch should be. Flick it on.

Jake is lying on the bed, arms straight at his sides, legs also straight. His eyes are open, staring into nothing. He's dressed in his SmokeHouse greens. His skin is grey.

I call his name again and again, then place a hand on his face. It is cool, but not cold. Not yet. I detect traces of a pulse. Very shallow breathing.

I look around. On the floor next to the bed is his med inducer. It is supposed to be impossible to overdo. But somehow people find a way. I wouldn't think Jake would, but who knows? I reach down and pick up the inducer. It is tube-shaped. About the size of a human finger. On one side is a square that will darken when the inducer is empty.

This one is. Used up.

I look at Jake's face again. He really needs help. I know little about how to help him, though. First aid is not in my training. So do I use his vid? Call the authorities? I see no other way.

Except that might expose me too.

I shake my head. No, it will be all right. I'll leave before they come.

I straighten, planning to return the living area, when I hear something else. A creak, coming from somewhere outside. Possibly near the front door.

My collector instincts snap into focus. I crouch and move slowly to the hall. I hear a familiar sound.

Then I see it: a collector's monitor, hovering at the edge of the living room. It is slowly turning. Scanning the area.

I know the capabilities of these machines. There is no way to escape, no way to duck back in time.

I watch the monitor hover. The system is in play. The system cannot be broken.

I slowly get to my feet. Raise my hands.

Twenty seconds later, a collector steps into view. Male, certainly, and thicker than me. More compact. For all other intents and purposes, it could be me. Solid black mask over the face, matching black suit. All the gadgets in their proper spots. Tranker cinched to each wrist.

"You are not Jake Braden." The mask's voice is mid-range but slightly mechanical. Modified by the mask.

"No, I'm not." He doesn't know who I am. I have to remember that. Only Quantum does, but *she* won't be telling. I nod toward the bedroom. "Jake's a friend." I think that's right. I think he's a friend. So, what else would a friend say? "He needs help. He's in there."

The mask approaches slowly and waves his right hand over me. Weapon scan. I see his posture relax when he doesn't find anything. My decoder doesn't register as dangerous, I know. I've checked at home.

"Step out into the living room," he says, directing me with

his arm. I do so, and he creeps down the hall into the bedroom. I know what he sees. What he thinks. He's registering that, aside from the complication of me being here, his job just got easier.

Jake got voted? What are the probabilities? The odds? I stare at that empty wrapper on the coffee table again. Three in the same family?

Of course, maybe his ex and son weren't. Maybe something else happened.

The mask returns to the hall. I know the call has already been made. That the white van is on its way. What that ultimately means for Jake.

I shrug. What can I do?

"Thank you for your assistance, Radial Crane. It will be factored into your vote matrix."

I nod and look sheepishly at the floor. I glance toward the front of the house. Through the windows, I can see that the van has already arrived. White and nondescript. Could be the same one that did pickup duty for me. I frown. Jake won't even get to see the fancy inside. Not in his state.

The mask walks past me to the front door. Opens it. "Your presence is no longer needed." He motions again with his arm. Waving me home.

I try to decide what a civilian might say. The inane chitchat I've heard over the years. I remember the aquarium to my left. Nod that direction. "Someone needs to feed his fish," I say.

The collector doesn't even flinch. "We have people who take care of the details. Clean-up people. All pets will be protected. Preserved."

I force a smile. "Yeah, no one ever voted a pet, right?"

The mask says nothing. Only looks at me. I know what he's factoring, though. Danger potential. Resistance quotients. Quietly asking for my history.

Quantum will filter, of course. The mask will hear about my SmokeHouse job, the location of my parents and family. Law violations. But any vote weights will be completely contrived. A complete figment. Collectors don't get voted.

Through the open door, I can see two men exit the van. Both wearing white suits and hoods that obscure their eyes. The first wave of the cleanup crew. Primarily used to remove inactive incons. Which Jake is.

I throw a glance at the hall. Toward the room where Jake lays. I resist shaking my head. This can't be happening. This twinge of guilt, of apprehension. The mask is me.

Finally, I force a shrug. "Okay, I'm going." I move toward the door. The mask is watching every step. Surveying. Calculating. Making sure I'm not a problem. Soon he'll be off to his next job. His next collection. But this one needs to be soundly finished first.

As I pass him, I get this sudden urge to do something. To inhibit him in some way. It is an odd feeling. Unexpected. Like a portion of my heart broke off and sailed into a mist of an uncharted sea. I shrug the feeling away. It isn't right. Isn't good.

Plus, it is dangerous. I am the mask. The mask is me.

I walk down the sidewalk, give a smiling wave to the cleanup crew, step around the van, and go to my car. I don't look back.

CHAPTER

One night later I am again in my apartment, vidscreen on, volume on low, baseball game noiselessly playing out. The Aquas are up to bat, Juan Yuvia at the plate. Yuvia is generally Hispanic in appearance, but there's a touch of something else——Japanese, I'm guessing—in his genetic makeup. He has a rigid, upright stance. Very polished. Professional. Looks like he means it.

The count is two and one. The pitcher is a rookie with an arm like a cannon, even if the cannon can't be aimed. Occasionally the ball finds its way into the strike zone, and then it is unhittable. A veritable blur.

The stadium is about half full. The Aquas aren't having that great of a year. They'll get team voted eventually, I'm sure. Then we"ll be left with only one team in the area.

The screen flickers, then does it customary collector-summons dance. I rise from the couch and glance out the window. It is raining again. A steady drizzle. I frown. I still feel off. A little self-involved. Not ready to respond to the summons yet.

I walk up the hall to the bathroom. It is average too. Off white, light brown trim. The shower curtain is country blue with hints of green. The floor is white tile with that same blue as an accent color. The medicine cabinet is built into the wall to the left of the mirror. I open it and retrieve my med inducer. It is standard issue, only for keeping things even. I rarely use it. Tonight I think it's time. Meds aren't supposed to affect reaction time, thought patterns, but I'm superstitious about that.

I'm off. Still not right. Got to snap free.

Quantum is expecting me to call. My presence is needed. My skills.

I put the inducer to my throat and press the button. Feel the instant euphoria. Count to ten. The molasses in my head seems to clear. I nod. Return the inducer to its place. Check myself in the mirror. Run a quick hand through my hair. Trace the hints of grey at the edges. The advent of age.

Enough ruminating. Go!

Ten minutes later, I'm at the pickup point. The dark van arrives and I enter. "Where am I off to, Quantum?" I ask into my mask.

"Mercer Isle. Quadrant six."

I nod. Affluence, then.

The door slides shut, and we're in motion.

Mercer Isle is covered by a projected synthbow—an ionic screen designed for localized weather control. The Isle is the only place in PacNorth that gets rain when they schedule it. If the screen is in place when it rains, the moisture gets redirected into Lake Wash. Nice for the city, bad for anyone who happens to be fishing that day.

Twenty minutes later, the van stops, the door opens, and I exit. It is a suburban neighborhood, the houses are mostly brick and massive, filling nearly their entire lot. Massive houses piled on top of each other. Separated by rows of trees, or in some cases, decorative fences. The house we're parked by appears to be the nicest. The driveway is circular, composed of paver stone, with a large "W" as part of its design. It is outlined with lights. There is a small, drooping willow tree in the center of the circle. Immaculate bushes. The house is made of grey stone.

I can't help but look up. The ion screen is in place. Instead of clouds overhead, there appears to be a clear, dark sky. There also seems to be stars, though I have no idea if the constellations are correct. Given the context, they probably are.

"House number two-three-one," Quantum whispers. "The incon is inside. She's low risk. A minor."

I scowl. My calls are supposed to be adults or high-risk teens. Low risk is for the snatch-and-grab squad. Nannies with nets. It isn't what I need tonight. With the way I feel.

"They're waiting for you," Quantum says.

They, right. There'd be another family member involved. The primary caregiver.

I make another scan of the house. It looks like a place someone could be happy in. Supportive. Almost a castle, really. A far distance from my standard-yet-polite apartment. I contemplate bringing out a monitor to do a quick buzz over. Make sure things are as smooth as Quantum says.

I check the houses on both sides. Though there is some distance between, in this neighborhood a transport van will be noticed. Plus, there's the streetlights: high-end, pure biological light bars. They are plentiful.

I notice a window blind move on the house to my right. A blind is pulled up on the house ahead then. Over the garage. In the room usually called the bonus room.

I take the sidewalk toward the house. Ahead, the walk joins and blends into the circle drive, then it emerges on the other side to finish at the house's front porch. The night is quiet. I detect only the faint murmurs of vidscreens being watched. I smell a heavy scent of flowers. I notice a blooming bush in the circle as I pass.

I'm about ten steps from the front door when it swings open. Standing there is a woman in her early thirties. Straight, brown hair neatly pulled back into a ponytail. She is wearing stylish beige pants and a matching long-sleeved shirt. She crosses her arms. Her face looks hard but conflicted. There's some twitching under the surface. "Finally, you're here," she says.

I nod, feeling a bit confused. Typically, people don't welcome us in. "Who is this?" I ask Quantum.

"The incon's mother," Quantum says.

I frown. I hate family issues. Hate the emotion of it.

Still frowning, I reach the front door. The woman backs into the house, pushing the door along with her. I get a tweak in my stomach. A little biological foreshadowing, perhaps. Something doesn't feel right.

The interior of the house is immaculate. Tastefully decorated. Like a museum. The entranceway floor and that of the adjoining living area is white granite. The trim is painted light green. The walls are white but filled with decoration. There are oil paintings of important historical events and figures, along with color matched paintings of scenery and wildlife. Intermixed are family photos. A hodge-podge of subject matter, but somehow it all seems to work together, matching in color and theme. Someone spent a lot on a decorating adviser, I'd guess.

To the left of the living area is a large office. It is trimmed in solid wood, medium stain, with lots of grain. There is a large matching desk and two walls filled with paper books. Another historical touch. There's a model of a cannon on one of the shelves. Bronze. To my right is a wide spiral staircase. It is carpeted with a rose and green pattern. Plush and remarkably clean-looking. There are family portraits along the wall beyond it.

The woman moves ahead of me, then points up the stairs. "She's up there. Please make this quick."

The vote is the vote. I don't dispute it. Don't laud it. But this particular job…isn't me. I try to keep my senses in focus. Searching for whatever can go wrong. But again, I feel that hollowness in my stomach. A reaction to the meds?

I climb the stairs. The family portraits show generations. Clustering of relatives, faces completely unknown to me. I see the hints of heredity. Similar eyes, similar broadness in a forehead here, small ears there. The links between father and son. Mother and grandmother.

Occasionally I see the image of the woman below me. Her with a female sibling. Her with her father. Her with someone I assume is a spouse or voter-approved lover. There are two children with her in one photo. A boy and girl. The girl is a younger version of the mother. Cheeks a bit more rounded. Face more full.

Is this who I'm here for?

I glance at the woman again. Study her features. Maybe it is an old picture. Maybe the girl is a delinquent now.

I reach the top floor. The carpeting changes to the green color from the stairs. The walls become less decorated. Simpler. Now it's game time. I feel as if I should crouch or prepare in some way. But I remain upright. The area to my left is open, overlooking the lower floor. To my right are three doors.

"Last door," the woman says from below.

"Quantum, why do I have this job?" I've done low impact collections before. Better than one a week. But tonight? Don't want it. Regardless of how I usually feel, I need action now. An opponent. Anything to keep the memory of Jake's collection far away. Where it is supposed to be.

"I only distribute the resources, Radial. You know that."

I swear. Quantum says nothing.

I approach the last door on the right. It is open. It appears to be a child's room. There are colorful pictures on the wall visible from the hallway.

I shake my head. This is definitely snatch and grab territory. I shouldn't be involved with this. Below my training.

I stand in the doorway. There are bunk beds here. Both made. Neat. Comforters of a cartoon character. An animated frog. The top bunk is empty, but sitting on the lower bunk is a girl, roughly ten years of age. Blond hair, combed straight. Her back is against the wall. Her body and face are turned perpendicular to me. She is partially hidden by the shadows of the upper bunk. Both her arms and legs are crossed.

I expect a fight. She has to know what this is about. What my presence means. But aside from a cursory glance, she doesn't even look at me. Simply stares forward. I'm not sure what to do. How to proceed.

"A girl, Quantum?"

"That is your collection. Darcy Medal. Yes."

I think of the woman downstairs. The immaculate house. How could anything be so wrong that she'd vote *this* child? Today.

"This is S&G work. I don't want it. Not tonight."

There is a pause. "Make good your charge."

I snort and shake my head. Maybe the girl will turn out to be troublesome. Mean. Then I won't care as much.

Care? I never care! I'm the mask.

I move around so I can look the girl—the incon—in the face. It is completely expressionless. A mask of her own. I enable my external speakers. "You have been ruled an incon," I say. "You must come with me." I feel the trankers itching at my wrists. Seeming unnecessary now. Heavy.

The girl only sits and waits. Her eyes rarely blink as they look at me. Previously, I would've simply grabbed her and thrown her over my shoulder. Carried her out. I stoop as if to do that, but I feel resistance in my arms. I rest on my haunches for a moment. Watching her. "Don't make me carry you," I say finally.

She extends her legs and slides out to the edge of the bed. Her arms remain crossed. Her eyes are fixed on my mask. I feel strangely self-conscious, as if she can see my face. The real me.

"Where are you taking me?" she asks.

"To a collection point."

She stands. "Where I'll die?"

I stay silent. Unsure how to answer. I don't think about what happens after delivery. It isn't my problem. My job. I get the incon to the white van. That's what I do. I'm a collector.

Just like Jake. His family.

But I didn't collect Jake. Or his family.

I shake my head. It doesn't matter. Stay focused. Do the job.

"Are you okay?" Darcy—no, the *incon*—asks.

"Come on," I say, straightening. I back up so she can walk out in front of me.

"Mom doesn't want me anymore," she says. "Says I'm too much trouble."

Stay silent. I must stay silent. Technically there is no way her mother's vote alone would be sufficient. I know enough about Quantum's weights and counterweights to know that. The formula is fair. Just. Based on many things. Many votes. Parents' votes carry *heavy* weight for their children, though. Always have.

An odd thing happens. Instead of stepping in front of me, the girl reaches for my hand. Grasps it.

I quickly pull away, motion again that she should precede me. But my stomach churns. I think of Jake and his son, Brian. The start of my current misgivings. I don't like it. I scowl beneath the mask. Shake my head. "Go on," I say. "I'll follow you."

She shrugs and quietly moves ahead. I notice her feet. They have on only pink stockings. She'll need shoes. She should have shoes, right?

We walk into the hallway. I notice the chandelier that hangs out over the living area below. It must have hundreds of lights. It is turned off. Other lights light the hallway and the downstairs. I drift toward the upstairs railing and can see the mother standing below. Waiting. Arms crossed.

I hate straight domestics. I shouldn't be here.

Mask. Be a mask. Granite.

We reach the stairs. Begin our descent. The girl's eyes seek her mom and find her. Mom's arms are crossed still too. I think it helps her hold things in. It is like a tourniquet of the heart. For both of them.

"If Dad was here, he wouldn't let you," the daughter says.

Mother glares and shakes her head. Looks at me. "This is taking too long. Can't you just carry her out?"

I remain silent. Better to not get involved. As long as the incon is moving on her own, there is no reason to interfere. To create a ruckus. Usually young ones aren't like this, though. Usually they don't go easily. Not without a show of some emotion. Anger or fear.

Darcy must be up to date on her meds. Children usually get them covertly. In their favorite treats.

The front door is still open. No one speaks as we exit. I notice the slice of manicured lawn that runs to my left in front of the house. Even in the dark I can tell it is full and green. Immaculate. I see the white van enter the circle driveway from the far side. It circles around, partially hidden by the bulk of the weeping willow. It reaches the edge of the sidewalk. The incon waits.

The van's side door opens, revealing the heavily carpeted interior, the screen hung on the wall that separates and protects the driver, the plush seating.

The incon gives the van a once over. Her arms are crossed. She turns to look at me. "Will you ride with me?"

CHAPTER 11

It is an unusual request. Sometimes collectors ride along to restrain, but that isn't the incon's decision. We're not the person they want to see before delivery.

"I typically don't," I say, "but it's allowed." My stomach hopes she doesn't want it, though. I want to move on to the next job. A real job.

She stares at me. Frowns. "I want you to."

I nod. "Incon requests ride along," I say to Quantum.

"Confirmed."

"Who are you talking to?" the incon asks.

"It isn't important," I say and move her toward the van opening.

She steps into the van, and I follow. The door draws closed, sealing away the outside. Bringing a new level of silence.

The girl sits back in her seat and tucks her legs beneath her. I'm amazed by her bravery. Her lack of response. Again, I suspect meds.

I'm thinking too much about Darcy, about the incon. Too much empathy is a bad thing. I'm supposed to push those thoughts away. Make a ball of them and throw them far.

The van begins to move. I'm overwhelmed by a sense of

discomfort. A need to get away. A wave of motion sickness. I wish for another med induction. Something to even things out again.

What is wrong with me?

My mind drifts to Jake's body. The presence of that other mask.

The vote is fair. The vote is just. The system works! It is what preserves us.

I am the mask. The mask is me.

"Are you fully operational, collector?" Quantum says.

Her emotional prodding surprises me. "Yes," I whisper. "Operational."

There is a pause. "Your biometric readings are within tolerances," she says then. "Remain focused. Complete your charge."

I smile within the mask. "Of course."

"Do you have a daughter?" the girl asks.

I shake my head. "I can't comment on personal affairs. I am a collector. That's all you can know." I stare at the mounted vid screen. It is on a shopping channel. A woman is holding up a fancy piece of jewelry shaped like a dolphin. "Sorry."

The girl kneads her hands together nervously, then looks out the darkened window. "It's okay…"

Is it? Is it all okay? What I do?

It's essential. The population. The process.

I check the mask's chronometer. Less than an hour has passed. Feels longer. And now a ride to the collection point. I haven't been to one in months. It is rarely necessary. No one *asks*.

Until today.

Ten minutes later, we enter the I-90 freeway, headed east. On our right, beyond the sprawl of suburbia, mountains dominate. The foothills of the Cascades. Green all the way up. I know juvenile incons tend to go to the outlying facilities. We must be headed for one of those.

"Collector, do you think there's a God?"

The question startles me. Partly due to med aftereffects, I think. Still…it is an unusual question. In effect, god—every god—was voted out long ago. Now they're only brought out on special occasions. Like colored frosting on a cake. By politicians. And occasionally athletes.

"That isn't my concern," I say.

The incon frowns. "Right. Just doing your job…taking kids away."

"I collect incons. And sometimes deliver them. That's all. It's the way it works."

She nods. "By a vote, right? Everything decided by a vote."

"Correct."

She looks out the window again. Gazes at the nearest foothill, Tiger Mountain. At the top, the pine trees have a dusting of snow. "But what if the voters are wrong?" she asks. "That's possible, isn't it?"

No. Voting is the only standard we have. A remnant of the old Union. Her questions echo Jake, though. *His* questions. The system.

"The system is correct," I say, but feel sorrow in the statement. "It is all we have."

She shrugs, looks at the hills. "All we have…"

I study the foothills too. It is easier than looking at her face. Less complicated.

"I wanted to be a nurse," she says. "My dad said I would make a good nurse."

I continue to look outside. Try not to listen.

"My brother used to hide things—scary things—in my closet. Rubber spiders, bats, and things. To try to make me scream before bed. Collector, are you listening?"

I glance at her. She's leaned forward, legs crossed, hands together. "Yes," I say.

"Even large, scary masks. Things with teeth and blood." She shrugs. "You know, masks. Like yours."

I nod.

"But my dad, he would always check my closet for me before bed. And he had a baseball bat he would carry…"

I grit my teeth to keep the feelings out. Yet she continues with her story. Her dad protecting her. Acting as her shield.

Soon mountains surround us on both sides. No longer foothills. Mountains. Made of stone. Towering rocks jutting out of forested pine. More snow. And strength. Permanence.

The girl stares at the scenery. "We used to come this way all the time," she says. "To ski the pass. Before it closed."

I nod. I remember skiing here as a child. Though by no means the most challenging or consistent of the local ski resorts, it had the advantage of being nearby.

Somehow, the vote got it. A handful of people hurt. Poor food in the restaurants. Something. "Yes," I say. "Too many negs."

I watch the mountains. Eventually I notice an old railway span. A metal bridge between one mountain and the next. It was converted into a bicycle trail some time ago. As far as I know, *that* is still open.

The van shifts into the right lane. I hear the click of directional signals. Ahead is an off-ramp, which the driver veers toward. The terrain beyond it is thick with pine trees. There is no sign of civilization whatsoever. No fueling station or restaurant. Only thick, green forest. It feels especially dense in the dark. Only a lone streetlight illuminates the intersection.

"Spooky." The girl reaches for my hand, but I decline the contact. She looks at me. Stares. I notice wetness in her eyes now.

I am not for this. I reach down and adjust the trankers on my wrists. Straighten myself. Try to shake away the feeling.

The van turns to the right. We enter a lonely road with only an occasional streetlight to give a glimpse of the forest around us. Ten minutes pass.

The lights of the North Bend facility become apparent on our right. It is brick construction, rust colored, three stories high. Looks like a misplaced office building from one of the area's tech firms. There is little landscaping here. Only a solid grey parking area and a circular drive. There is another white van exiting the facility. Neither van pauses to acknowledge the other. The system is cold.

We reach the drop off point near the glass, front doors. Those doors opens, and two large men in white come out.

Their faces are obscured, but not like mine. Their masks are more like that of surgeons, with their eyes still visible. Something about that bothers me. I never noticed it before, but today, in this instant, that little exposure troubles me. Each man has, in his hand, a short meter-long whip, colored green. A stunlash.

"Are you still fully operational, collector?"

"Yes, Quantum," I say. "I'm fine."

The van door slides open. I'm hit with the scent of heavy ozone. Air infused with a trace of pine. There is a low hum in the background, emanating from the building. I can also hear the sound of a nearby waterfall. Crashing and roaring.

I step out and turn for the girl. This time I offer her my hand. She stares at it a long time, but then takes it. She scoots forward and out. The "doctors" are still five meters from us. They grip the handles of their lashes lightly, holding them at their hip. They don't expect trouble.

"A van will be there to pick you up in five minutes," Quantum says.

I acknowledge. Another job in the queue. The night is young.

The doctors hold out their hands. Now in front of me, the girl—Darcy—sort of cowers into me. I feel her shiver. Taste her nervous fear.

I look at the men. Sense their emotional detachment.

I think of Jake. And his son and missing ex. And the approaching black van, soon to take me on another collection.

I feel Darcy's presence. Her cowering into me. Her need for a shield.

Can you help me, Radial? It has blood in it.

And something breaks.

CHAPTER

As the doctors take Darcy's arms, pulling her to them, she lets out this chirp of a scream. I sense the white van behind us beginning to roll away. I step back, then find myself crouching into attack position. The girl struggles. The doctors are distracted, trying to manipulate and control her. One raises his stunlash, and begins to bring it down.

My tranker fires. Her attacker drops to the ground. Twitching. Rendered unconscious.

Darcy and the other doctor grow silent and still. The doctor looks at me. First in confusion, then in recognition. He releases the girl and swings the stunlash my direction. I dive to the right to avoid the lash striking my left side. I impact the ground, then roll again as the lash hits the sidewalk near me.

A siren blares. I sense the delivery van stopping again. Hear the driver exiting. He will have a larger weapon. A lethal weapon. I quick-fire my other tranker and catch the second doctor at the hip. I hear him yelp and the *crunch* of his fall to the pavement.

I look at Darcy. She has a hand across her mouth. Her eyes are wide, looking first at the doctors and then at me. Her eyes widen more. She raises the other hand, points.

I swivel, turn, and react.

The driver is five steps from me, dressed similar to the doctors on the ground. In his hands is a large double-barreled weapon. Projectile gun, doubtless. Not tiny darts like my tranker, but killing rounds. Death in a finger press.

I squat to my haunches and position myself to block the girl.

The driver raises the weapon, levels it at my head. "Stop!" he yells. His trigger finger compresses.

I free a monitor from my hip. It hisses in my hands, the built-in engines beginning to fire, then reorient.

The driver's eyes shift, distracted by the new sound. I pitch the monitor his direction. His gun discharges, shattering the monitor into a dozen pieces. The remains shower the sidewalk around me.

Darcy screams again.

I launch at the driver, at his gun. I get under it, then hug his legs. I pull him down, and raise my right hand to trank-fire at close range. He goes out like a rookie batter. Startled and confused.

I regain my feet and grab the girl's hand. Pull her with me.

"What are we—"

A gunshot stops her. It came from behind, from the direction of the facility. I don't look back. I push the girl ahead of me. Toward the white van that still sits idling.

We skirt around the front to additional gunfire. I throw her into the front seat, she scrambles to the passenger side, and I climb in behind her. The door closes.

I take a moment to survey the controls. They are similar to my personal vehicle's, excepting one thing: There is a heavy duty security system. Much stronger than the one on a typical passenger vehicle. I stomp on the foot pedal, but the engine doesn't even change in pitch. I rock the steering wheel. Nothing.

I glance out Darcy's window. There is a group of five men in white running toward us. Some carry stunlashes and large silver shields. Others carry long, black firearms.

"What are you doing?" Darcy is focused on me. "You can't take me back home! I was voted."

I stare at her. Fact is, I don't know what I'm doing. Certainly nothing I was trained for. Nothing I'm *supposed* to do.

"Collector!" Quantum squawks. "There are warnings from your quadrant. What has happened?"

I bring out my decoder. I grip its oval form in my hands and try not to think. Only act. I sweep it over the vehicle's console, let it do its work. The small face flashes red. I swear.

A round of gunshot hits the van behind Darcy. She screams and ducks. The ducking is good. She should've been doing that all along. But the screaming? That is a little much. It causes me to fumble the decoder. Drop it to the floor.

"Please hurry," she whimpers.

I feel around for the decoder and find it centimeters from my left foot. I bring it up and sweep it again. The face goes green, and the steering wheel gives a little wiggle.

It is free.

I smash the accelerator, and we jolt ahead with all the speed the bio engine can give us. Another round hits the back of the van, but aside from the sound, there is no damage. These machines are made to take a beating. Any collection could bring resistance, after all.

There is a large *bang* as I drift onto the circle drive's sidewalk. I swear and correct, bringing us back on smooth pavement. There are more muffled gunshots. Yelling.

In seconds we are out on the road again. The sirens start to fade. I check the side mirrors for pursuit, but see none. Someone stealing a white van isn't expected. Neither is rescuing an incon.

Is that what I've done?

We round a forested bend, and the collection point disappears from the rearview mirror. I almost begin to relax, but then I see the dark shadow of a collector van approaching us. My ride.

Will the driver notice that a mask is driving a delivery truck? I crouch so only my eyes are over the wheel. I tell Darcy to hide herself completely, which she does. I hold my breath as the black van approaches, draws alongside, then passes. I accelerate as it drives around the bend.

Did my old life just pass me by? A funny thought. The symbolism.

I glance at Darcy. She's still huddled beneath the passenger dash. "You can come up now," I say.

She does so, eyes wide. "Where are we going?" she asks. "Why did you do that?"

I'm not sure, so I don't answer. I see the on-ramp for the highway approaching. I contemplate whether to head east into the wilderness, or west into the city.

The former would require preparation. Training I don't have. We'd encounter desolation, wild beasts, and fire.

But the latter? Millions of people. Thousands of enforcement officials. Hundreds of masks.

We can't stay in this van, regardless. It is a dead giveaway.

"What has happened?" Quantum asks. "Who are you talking to?"

Speaking of giveaways…

I check the mirror and slow, bringing the van to the side of the road.

"Why are you stopping?" Darcy asks.

"You didn't answer, collector," Quantum says. "Are you stopped?"

I shake my head. "I'm having some difficulty. Mask is itching. I'm taking it off."

"Don't do that, Radial."

I look at the girl. Can I trust her with my face. My real face?

I raise a finger, hoping she gets the message. I indicate her eyes and point to her window.

Darcy stares, still trying to figure me out. After a few seconds of pointing, she finally turns and looks away.

I wrench the mask off. Built into the internal surface near the chin is a black ribbon of integrated circuitry. It contains the components that relay my voice to Quantum, and my position. I tear that out and toss it out the window. It flutters in the wind. I push the mask back on.

I start the car moving again. Head it for the on-ramp into the city.

"Okay," I say.

Darcy looks back at me. "You sound different."

"I do? How?"

"More human. Less mechanical." She pulls a knee up and hugs it. "Can't you just leave your mask off?"

I shake my head. "It would be better if I didn't."

"Why?"

I frown to myself. "I don't know. But I think it is better."

She stares for a moment. "Are you one of those strangers I should be afraid of?"

I can't help but smile. The highway is sparse on traffic. I feel more free than I've ever been. But also exposed. Really exposed and lost. "Up until a few minutes ago, I was the stranger *everyone* should be afraid of."

She looks at the mountain on her side. It is about three quarters forest, homogeneous in appearance, except in the exact center is a large square swatch that is clearly younger growth. It is a place loggers cleared many years ago that has started to regrow on its own.

I give a passing thought to Heather Black. The blonde I met. Pretty. I wonder what she's doing? How would she feel about dating a rogue collector? Could I blame it all on my meds?

"Won't they chase us?" Darcy asks.

I look out my side window, first back and then up. My infraction has certainly been logged by now. "High speed chases were voted due to the risk to other commuters," I say. "Better to wait and watch. Give the perpetrator an instant neg and catch him later. Send someone like me."

Quantum is always watching, though.

I hear a low hum and get a sinking feeling. Again I check behind us. I see a glint of something in the sky.

Darcy has noticed too. "What's that?" she says.

I swear. "A traffic drone," I say. "Or worse."

The drone draws steadily closer. I hesitate, torn on what to do. If I accelerate, I assure detection. But If I don't?

There's another off-ramp ahead. It leads, I know, to a large suburban housing division. A planned community that has everything one might require. All pretty and polite. Plenty of people, plenty of commuters—which means plenty of private vehicles. With another glance at the rearview mirror, I move toward the off-ramp.

The drone hovers directly behind us. I expect it to take a more aggressive stance. To move up and flash a warning. Or slam the van into autodrive. Was that what it was sent to do? I fight to keep from speeding.

"Will it stop us?"

I ignore her question. I try to ignore the emotion of it all, but it is difficult.

Suddenly, the drone accelerates and veers off west toward the greater metropolitan area. I drive incredulously for a few moments, then laugh out loud.

"It left," Darcy says. "Why did it leave?"

I wave a hand over my torso. "Must be my suit," I say. "It creates a dead spot." I can hardly believe it, though. Our luck. I'm way outside the norm here. New calculations will have to be made.

"So, now what?"

I chuckle again. "First," I say, "we find another car."

"Where?"

I tap the decoder. "Anywhere we can."

She nods. "And after that?"

The light at the bottom of the off-ramp is green. We move on through. "After that..." I shake my head, shrug.

"God only knows," she says.

I look at her, and she gives me a half smile. "It is something people used to say."

I snort. "If you say so," I say. "God only knows."

CHAPTER

A half hour later I've secured another vehicle—a black SUV bio—mostly because the color felt comfortable, but also because they are commonly driven by adolescents and soccer moms, and I am neither.

I miss the indestructibility of the delivery van, though. Our new car won't stop bullets.

I also manage to get us something to eat. There is a SmokeHouse drive-thru nearby, still open, which accepts the free meal vouchers I've earned. That means I didn't have to reveal my identity. I'm thankful the whole process is automated. Never had to show my face. Not even when the food came through the window dispenser.

I park in the parking lot of a local business, a place that I know doesn't have many night patrols. It is the best I could think of. The building's security lights are out of range, and a nice row of pine trees shields us from the nearest road.

I place my to-go box on the floor and the other on Darcy's lap. Hers is white and brown with a cartoon cowboy on one side and a happy cow on the other. She stares at it.

"It's chicken," I say. "You like chicken, right?"

She doesn't move. Only her eyes look my direction.

"Every kid likes chicken."

She sags a bit, then studies the grey console in front of her.

"What is it?" I ask. "There are fries there too. I got you milk."

She gives a quick shake of her head. I notice the hint of moisture in her eyes. A coming mist. "I don't want to eat," she whispers.

I have little experience with adolescent girls outside the SmokeHouse. "You're not hungry?"

She crosses her arms and shakes her head. Tears slide down her cheek. Some land on her forearms. Then her body begins to heave, and little sobs come out. Her hand reaches for the door handle. "I want to go," she says.

Probably she was medicated. Probably those are wearing off now like mine are. Except I actually feel better. "Want to go where?" I ask. "Back to the facility? Back to the mom who voted you?"

She tosses the box aside, wrenches open the door, and sprints across the lot. And while I *could* let her go—make it easier on myself—I find myself running after her, scanning every direction as I go. I consider using the tranks. She nearly makes it to the road before I collect her.

I drag her back to the car, kicking and beating against my chest. I toss her into the seat, make sure the safety lock is on, and close the door again.

She responds by locking *my* door.

I again contemplate using my tranks.

I check our surroundings. I feel really nervous about being exposed. Anyone who saw this would find it strange. Anyone.

"Let me in, Darcy."

"Not until you take off your mask." She's perched in my seat, looking hard at me. Her eyes are red. Tears are still falling.

"I can't," I say.

"Why not?"

I bring out my decoder and raise it up where she can see it. I wave it over the door lock. It clicks open.

She looks surprised. "That's not fair!"

I wrench open the door. She retreats to her seat, and I climb in. "Don't do that again," I say.

"Why not?"

I shake my head, feel myself losing whatever empathy I had. That *could* be the meds. "Because we could be seen."

She collects her to-go box from the floor. Holds it. Doesn't open it. "Can I get a puppy?" she asks.

"A what?"

"A puppy. I'd feel better with a puppy." She wipes a tear away but opens her box and finally takes out a piece of chicken. It is a tad overcooked. Their fry guy was sleeping. She takes a bite anyway.

I watch as Darcy now devours her food. You would think it was her last meal. But in actuality, it is more like her first meal. Something about that feels good.

She notices me watching. "Are *you* going to eat?"

I shake my head. "Later."

She puts the chicken down. "You're going to keep your mask on?"

"For now," I say. "It's safer." Makes me feel safer anyway. The armor. The mask.

"You don't want me to see your face? You saved me from…" She nods toward the rear of the vehicle. "But you don't want me to see you."

"I don't," I say. "That's right."

She frowns and takes a bite of her chicken. She started with three boneless pieces. She has one to go. Boneless is safe, typically. But not at the rate she's eating it.

I can't help but smile.

"What now?" she asks. "Are you going to raise me? Take me to my soccer games?" She chews. "Even if *I* don't know who you are, they do, right? The people you talk to? In your helmet thingy?"

I nod. "She, um, *it* is called Quantum. It maintains the list of incons. Activates collectors."

"It? Is it automated? Like a robot?"

"An artificial intelligence. Sometimes I think of it as female, but it isn't really." I glance out the window. See no motion. I do notice a light in the sky. It is a few streets over, but it seems to be heading in our direction. Hopefully no one saw the collector chasing the little girl. "It is deep in the city somewhere."

"And that's what makes it fair, right? The fact that there's no person."

I nod and keep watching the light. Sometimes they do a street-by-street sweep. Look for any jaywalkers or defecating dogs.

She looks outside too. "So you can't go home either. You can't return to your base or whatever?"

I snort. "There's no base," I say. "I have a life. A normal life. An average place. An average job."

"So you could be anyone? Living anywhere? Wow, I could already know you!"

"Not likely. But my home will be watched. Can't go there."

I take an inventory of what I have with me. The weapons. Over a dozen tranker pellets. One functional monitor. A decoder. A laz burner. Seven lethal pellets, though they are harmless without Quantum authorization. It is enough for now. For whatever.

"So, where do we go?"

The light in the sky takes a turn our direction. I don't like that. Don't like to be seen. I sit up in my seat. Start the car. "We need to go."

She's on her fries now. One dangles in her hand. "Go where?"

"I have an idea."

CHAPTER

Fifteen minutes later, we're standing on Jake's porch. It is nearly midnight. I am tired, and I'm sure Darcy is as well. The SUV is parked around the corner in a small commuter lot. Already there is a house-for-sale sign in Jake's front yard. There is a dim light inside that occasionally flickers, but I know that's a trick. Both it and the sign are part of the cleanup-crew's job. There is doubtless a security dog inside too. It'll bark if I open the door. But it's only for show—no biting. I hope.

"Who lives here?" Darcy asks.

"It's a friend's place," I say. "We'll be safe here for a while."

"Does your friend know who you are? What you are?"

I shake my head. I bring up the decoder and pass it over the door lock. As before, it clicks free. I push it open, and wait. No sound. I take a step inside and notice the still-lit aquarium. The couch. The food wrappers have been removed from the coffee table. Probably cleaner inside now than it ever was. When Jake was—

I get this sharp pain in my gut. Push it away.

"Maybe there's no dog yet..."

I step fully into the house and turn to motion Darcy in. I hear a scratching noise to my left, and stop. A silver canister rolls around the corner from the kitchen. On its top is a slowly spinning portion, complete with a blue, electronic eye. The *dog*. It must've been in one of the bedrooms. Far enough that it didn't hear me enter. I push Darcy back outside, and slipping to the floor, crawl slowly to the cover of the couch.

The dog notices the slightly ajar door and makes a hurried roll toward it. Its mimicry software kicks in, producing a loud, angered growl. It is impressively real sounding. The bot rolls around the coffee table and past my position. Heads straight for the door.

Folded on the edge of the couch is a thick blanket. I slide it off and bring it up.

The bot stops. The top portion swivels my way.

I throw, and manage to cover the entire thing. I fall on the bot, constrain it, and pick it up. It is surprisingly light for its size. Lots of plastics in its construction. The barking intensifies, becoming so shrill I can hardly stand it.

Darcy steps into the house.

"Shut the door," I hiss.

I drag the squirming dog to the aquarium and drop it in. The bot struggles, water splashes everywhere, but eventually the barking ceases. Then the movement. The eye light continues to shine.

Darcy's eyes go wide. "You drowned it," she says, as if it was a live pet.

"It was the best way," I say. "If it's a newer model, it's already reported us, and we'll have to leave." I check the bottom of the dog, between its foot treads. Read the numbers. "It's not. But it could've been."

"You killed the fish too," she says.

I step back and squint at the aquarium. It is about three quarters full of mechanical dog. "Not all of them," I point out a darting yellow. "There's one still swimming."

"But he'll probably die too." She puts a finger on the aquarium's side. "Look, some of the fluids are leaking out. You could've used the sink." She frowns. "Your friend will be mad."

I make a halfhearted scan of the kitchen behind me. Even in semidarkness, it appears cleaner than it was. No dishes on the counter. The sink gleams. The house is ready to be sold. To be reoccupied. And so it is.

"Fine," I say. "I'll move it." I hoist the dog, blanket and all, and walk into the kitchen. The burden is heavier now, and seemingly more awkward. Water drips all over the polished, wooden floor. I take two slow steps, slip, correct myself, then finally reach the stainless sink. I sit the dog in, bottom hanging over the side. It is the only way it will fit.

Darcy turns on the kitchen light. She looks at me, then at the now-soaked floor. "Big mess." Her hands find her hips, and she shakes her head.

I almost laugh. "You could find a towel," I say.

She begins to look through the kitchen cupboards, eventually finding one full of dishtowels. She drops a handful on the ground and moves them with her left foot. A lackluster attempt.

I leave her and walk down the hall to the bedrooms. I give them a cursory inspection. Both are clean and neat. Much of Brian's stuff seems to have been removed. There is now only enough to make it *seem* like a child's room. A large stuffed bear on the bed. A Mariners pennant on the far wall. A poster of Superman. The situation is the same in Jake's room. It is no longer his room, it is simply an adult's room. Any adult. The *next* adult.

I hear a noise behind me. I spin and see Darcy standing in Jake's doorway. "Your friend got collected, didn't he?"

I nod and straighten myself. My stomach grumbles. I clench my hands over it.

"Did you do it?"

I shake my head. "Someone else."

She nods, points across the hall. "Can I sleep in there?"

"Yes, that's a good idea." I step forward, causing her to retreat a little. "I'm going to eat and watch the street. Make sure that dog didn't report anything." I move into the hall and head for the kitchen.

"Collector?"

"Yes?" I say, still looking away.

"Thanks," she says. "For saving me."

I nod once. That impulsive act has changed my life forever. I'm an inconvenience to someone now. We're both incons.

A few minutes later, I retrieve my now-cold SmokeHouse takeout from the SUV. I shut off all the lights in the house, excepting the aquarium light in the living room.

I sit in Jake's couch and put my feet up on the coffee table. For the time it takes me to eat—for those precious ten minutes or so—I remove my mask.

CHAPTER

I dream I'm back at the SmokeHouse. I have a grill full of meat that I'm slowly cooking.

A steak goes on, all purple and cold. There is a hiss as it touches the grill. A small pop of grease. Then the smoke begins. Only a tendril at first, but eventually there is more. Minutes later, the blood begins to bubble to the steak surface. The back side is cooking, but also hardening. Firming. Searing. I use my spats to flip it. There is another popping hiss, a bit of grease splatters. More smoke. Next I'll need to rotate it.

A rattle awakens me. My head snaps up and my eyes scan the room. It is still dark. Early morning, but dark. I'm wearing my mask. I rise and look out the nearest window. It is raining.

"Where are you, Radial?" Quantum's smooth feminine voice within my mask. I've disabled my broadcast to her, but not hers to me. Typically, she talks only during collections. But this is a special occasion. "If you come in now, we can solve this. We can work things out."

Yes, I bet she can.

I return to the couch and place a hand on the side of my mask. Waiting.

"You were wise not to go home, but you will be found.

Your name and possible whereabouts have already been distributed. Tonight, a collector will come for you. Please surrender yourself before then."

I growl. I contemplate removing the mask and stripping the lining along with the embedded speakers, but I relent. If Quantum wants to talk, let her. It might prove useful.

I check the built-in chronometer. It is six-thirty-seven.

"You're a favorite, Radial. I won't deny that. Exceedingly useful. The system is the people's choice. It has proven successful. We need collectors like you to maintain it. It takes time to reach your level of competency."

I smile and shake my head.

The kitchen light turns on. Darcy stands there in dark blue pajamas that have small, yellow spiders all over them. It is a one-piece, with only head, hands, and feet exposed. She notices me, glances down at herself, and shrugs. "It was all I could find. I was cold." She drifts toward the refrigerator. "Is there food here?"

"Typically they leave some," I say. "To make the house look lived in."

"Right." She opens the refrigerator door and extracts a quart container of what appears to be apple juice. She begins searching the cupboards for a glass.

All so mundane. Not like our situation at all.

"They want me back," I say.

Darcy takes a drink and looks at me, wiping her mouth with her sleeve. "How do you know?"

I tap the side of my mask.

She raises an eyebrow. "They talk to you?"

I nod. "I only listen."

She shakes her head. "You can't go back, can you? It's a trick."

I stand and stretch. "I'm a collector. That's what I do. This mask—" I touch my head again. "It defines me."

She moves closer. "You're not that now, though. You're something different. Something important."

"I am?"

"Yes, you *change* things."

I snort, mockingly. "You have big ideas for a child."

She moves into the living room and glances at the aquarium on her right. Two fish are still swimming there. Survivors. "I had a good teacher."

Again I snort. "Your mother?"

She frowns. "No, not her. Never her. She maintained me. Made sure I was in school."

"Then who?"

"I have an uncle. He's a little weird, but he's smart. He can make things. You should meet him."

I shake my head. "Quantum will be watching your relatives. Even your aunts and uncles."

I need to decide what to do next. There are few routes out of PacNorth. North to Canada is walled and heavily patrolled. South to CalAm—what's left of it—is nearly impassable. Lava and heavy ash storms. East used to be the easy way. But that has bears and wolves now. Large ones. No one goes east.

I think of Heather again. Strikingly beautiful. And happy!

She wouldn't know anything. Not the public. Not yet. Not if Quantum still wants me.

I'm not really an incon, am I? I only went a little random. Not unusual, under the circumstances. Quantum understands. She pays attention to my voice, my emotions. She sounded sympathetic.

I glance at the door, the front windows. I need to access my personal comms somehow. Not at my apartment—that will be watched—but somehow. See if Heather has tried to contact me. See if *anyone* has tried to contact me. Contact Radial, I mean.

Is today a work day? Will the SmokeHouse miss me?

"Collectors go out at night," I say, contemplating the floor.

Darcy looks at me. "What?"

I raise my head. "They'll come after us, but only at night. That's important. Means we have today."

She nods. "Choose today whom to serve."

"What?"

"Something my uncle taught me. It's from the Bible."

I frown within the mask. "Irrelevant and old. Inconvenient."

She stomps a foot. "You're mean, Collector."

"I'm a realist. We're in a—*I'm* in a situation that's uncharted."

Darcy looks at the aquarium again. "Did you feed them?" When I don't answer, she walks to the cabinet beneath it and begins searching the drawers. She finds a container of fish food and pinches out a serving. "You should rescue more," she says, spreading food over the water. The fish dart back and forth.

"I don't care about fish."

She rolls her eyes. "More *people*," she says. "Like me. The voted. The incons."

"The people chose the system," I say. "It can't be broken."

A frown. "Are votes always right?"

I glance at my emptied takeout box, still on the coffee table. "You asked me that before."

She shrugs. "You didn't answer."

I clench my fists. "Because it is ridiculous," I say. "Impossible. The votes are right. They have to be."

"So, what about your friend?"

Another gut ache. "Jake?"

She walks to the couch and sits down. "He might still be alive. You could rescue him."

Could Jake be sitting somewhere, waiting? I shake my head. "I don't know what goes on at the facilities. Or where they all are."

That's not completely true. I've know where *many* of the facilities are, and typically, deliveries are to the closest. Saves resources. The closest to Jake's house would be less than ten kilometers away. Except that one is being renovated. Most of the incons are being taken to the facility near Lake Wash. There's a converted dwelling there. Used to be owned by a tycoon. Complete with underground parking and service passages.

But to attack it? Alone?

"They wouldn't expect that, would they?" she says. "For you to show up."

I shake my head again. "They're like fortresses. Not everyone liked it when the vote started to impact them. *Their* family and friends. It took a while. But before that, there were protests. Small riots."

"What's a riot?"

"A group of people attacking a place or simply going crazy, breaking things, starting fires, looting." I try to remember the last time there was any unrest. "It has been awhile. Almost before my time."

Darcy sips her juice. "So maybe they got lazy. Maybe they don't watch anymore." She shrugs. "You got away with me."

My face begins to itch beneath the mask. I give it a couple of shoves. The itch disappears. "But it wasn't that easy. This would be harder." The mask is supposed to be itch free. Not always the case.

"You weren't planning to rescue me, right?" Darcy says.

"No."

"So next time you can plan. It'll be easier."

I shake my head. It is a crazy idea. "It can't be done."

She shrugs. "What else can we do? Unless you want to see my uncle?"

I watch the fish circle and dart. Animals trapped inside a cube. I had a job. I had the beginnings of a possible romantic coupling. Friends. An apartment. Baseball. What do I have now?

"We can't stay here much longer," I say. "Two nights, maximum. A property agent could show up at any time. Good thing it's late fall, otherwise we'd have to worry about groundskeepers. We need to move around. Or leave the sector somehow."

"So you're not going to find your friend?"

"I can't think of a way to do it. You can't just drive up to these places."

"But the white vans do. All the time. Maybe we could get one again."

I get an idea. A way to do what she is saying. But I don't like it. I'm not supposed to have those sorts of ideas. "Yes, they do. But I only have you. And you don't drive."

"So teach me."

I laugh out loud. It sounds funny through my suit, but I can't help it. "You're like ten years old. Too short. Too obvious."

"I'm eleven," she says.

I laugh again. "Whatever."

"But I know the controls. My dad let me try once." Both hands clench her glass. "I can do it!"

Only so much you can do inside an aquarium. You can hide inside the cave, you can circle looking for food…or you can die.

I check my mask chronometer. Nearly seven now. Collection time has been over for more than an hour. It is still fairly dark. Grey. Better for our vehicle. Best time to invade a facility. "Let's go," I say.

"So you'll teach me?"

"No," I say. "Find something to eat. We need to move."

CHAPTER

The roads are slow and hilly, but at this time of the morning they are quiet. The area surrounding the facility used to be residential. *Expensive* residential, like Mercer Isle. But the vote got the better of it. The will of the people. Now it is mostly large warehouses. Brown and green cinder blocks, yet with the requisite number of trees around them. Enough to partially hide their size. Blend them in.

This particular facility has meaning to the area. A history. So the structure survived. The original owner, now long passed, started a company in his youth. It made something that thousands of people wanted. It grew. Changed. But then it outgrew its usefulness. Became inconvenient. Disappeared. That's the way of things.

Darcy is seated in the passenger seat, dressed in clothes she salvaged from Brian's room—dark pants and a black shirt turned inside out to hide the bright orange emblem on the front. She doesn't look half bad. Especially given the circumstances. Little girl collector, minus the mask.

"What are you thinking?" she asks.

"The past," I say.

"Your past?"

I shake my head. "The meaning of it. The futility of the

present. It all fades. Becomes inconvenient. Lost and abandoned."

I slow near a stand of trees and park, while Darcy stares out the window. Lake Wash is still visible. It is placid this morning. There are boats out there, but the closest is in the middle of the lake—roughly a kilometer away. The nearest floating bridge is also visible. Light traffic there today.

The sky is grey, and there's a light misting of rain. Typical this time of year.

"Deep," she says.

"The lake?" I say. "Nearly thirty meters, in this area. Especially deep for an inland body of water. Deepest in the sector."

She shakes her head. "No, what you said. Deep thought."

"You think so?" I look at her. "How old are you again?"

She shrugs. "I like to read."

I chuckle. "Just restating reality, Darcy. No one can claim permanence. Everyone is at risk. Everyone expendable. A chasing after the wind."

She gets a thoughtful look. "I think that's in the Bible too. The 'chasing' part."

"I thought it was from a song." I check my pants and boots. They look clean. Operational. "Your uncle teach you that?"

She shrugs again and looks at the lake.

I check our surroundings. No moving vehicles. Few lights. Perfect.

"So are you renting a boat to get in?"

I shake my head. "No boats for me."

"And you're not driving."

"No."

She pulls her right sleeve low over her hand. Then the left. "But that would work, wouldn't it? Act like a delivery truck?"

I shake my head. "Too risky. A converted guest house serves as a guard shack near the entrance. Beyond that is a long drive, an underground parking garage, and a short bridge. All before reaching the main facility."

"And it used to be someone's home?"

I smile within the mask. "Yes, a massive home. Lots of wealth built it."

"So what's your plan?"

"I've heard there is a southern gatehouse near the lake. It has another entrance."

"But that will have security too, right?"

"Probably not as much. Not now." I lift my trank-enabled arms. "Plus I have my equipment." I nod toward the nearest stand of trees. "The ground slopes from there to the lake. I'll follow the fence until I get close. Then I'll enter."

"And you can climb the fence?"

"I can get over it, I think. Yes."

She gives me a plaintive look. "What do I do?"

"Wait here." I reach behind her seat and bring out a small broadcasting device. It is yellow and ribbon shaped. Meant to fasten to the side of a child's face. A low-end communicator. "I found this at Jake's house. It's tuned to one of the lowband channels my mask receives. You can call me if you need help."

"Can you talk back?"

I shake my head. "No, my transmissions are scrambled. But that's okay. You call, I'll come. We don't need to talk."

Her eyebrows rise. "But what if *you* need help?"

"I won't," I say. "And if I did, you couldn't help anyway."

There is long pause, and her eyes begin to moisten. "And what if you don't come back?"

I feel a twinge of guilt. I can't guarantee her safety. I shouldn't leave her at all, with only a lame backup plan. It isn't the way I like to go into battle. Not the level of comfort I like to feel.

I point to the SUV's chronometer. "It is seven nineteen now." I reach to the dial that controls the vehicle's autodrive feature. It has a child safety mechanism built in—a simple push and turn operation—that I disable. "This vehicle has full auto-drive." I indicate the screen on the dash. "You know your uncle's address, right?"

She nods, still looking tearful.

"You enter the address here. If I'm not back by eight, start the car and let it drive you to him. Your uncle will look out for you, right? He cares for you?"

She nods. "I think so. He wouldn't neg me, anyway."

I nod. "Okay, good. If something goes wrong and I don't come back, go to him. There's a chance the car will be noticed, but there's nothing I can do about that. Of course, they could be watching your uncle's place..."

"I'll stop the car early," she says. "A few blocks away. I know places to hide. I won't go until it looks safe."

I nod, feeling a little better. "We have a plan then. Not a great plan. But I don't have my usual resources handy."

Darcy's hand closes over the comm unit I'm holding. She takes it and tries to fit it to her face, still with her hands pulled into the shirt. Somehow she manages. "Okay," she says, wrapping her arms around her body. "I'm cold."

I open the door. Step out into the street. "Right. Stay in the car." I scowl at how parent-like that sounded. I move past the car and into the safety of the trees.

Time to work.

***

Ten minutes later, I'm near the southern end of the property adjacent to the facility. In times past, this was the site of a grand estate, but now it is only evergreen forest. A planned reclamation. We needed more trees.

The trees prevent me from seeing the lake itself, or the skyline of Green City beyond. (The city was called "Seattle" once. Voted!) The air smells fresh, though.

The facility property line is marked by a ten-foot-high cement barrier. I select the nearest tree I can find—a twenty-meter-tall cedar—and slap the sides of each of my calves. Crampons extend from the front of my boots. A similar adjustment extends spikes from the palms of my gloves. I check my surroundings again and begin to climb.

I ascend until the barrier is below and ahead of me. The tree isn't close enough, nor its branches strong enough, for me to simply drop over. But that doesn't matter. I glimpse the top of a roof on the other side. I'm close to where I need to be.

I climb farther, reaching a place about two meters above

the barrier. I can see the facility grounds now. The roof belongs to the rear gatehouse. It is a brown, sloping structure with a solid wall on this side. All of the lighting appears to be on the other side of the building. The door has to be on that side, as well. The north side.

The main facility is a much larger structure, and it is hundreds of meters away. I see the roofs of other structures, as well.

Thankfully, the day remains grey and damp. There are no signs of people.

I touch a trigger at my forearm. The movement secures a monofilament to the loaded tranker dart. It also sets the trank to anchor mode. Extends barbs.

I aim at a point between the barrier and the gatehouse, mindful of any obstructions. I fire the tranker, watch as the filament spools out behind it. An instant later, the dart impacts the ground, boring in like a mole. I test it, finding it firm. I cut the filament and wrap it around the tree behind me just above a branch. Tie it off. Test the tension.

I sling my legs over the string and ride it across the barrier and in. I drop to the ground with a soft thump. The grass is dampened with rain.

I check my surroundings. There is a smaller building closer to the lake than the gatehouse. Beyond that, I see Lake Wash, Green City, and a hint of the Olympic mountain range. A spectacular view.

I move between the two buildings, secure in the cover they provide. As I move north, I notice that the smaller building has a short fence that extends out a fair distance. It encloses a rectangular area. Within that fence is what appears to be a sports court. It is dull blue in color, and overgrown with weeds. A remnant of the facility's earlier life.

I reach an ancillary portion of the gatehouse. It is the same dull brown, with lots of windows. I crouch low to avoid those and make my way forward.

"I hope you're okay, Collector." Darcy's voice in my mask speakers. "Wish you could talk to me." She pauses. "I'm okay."

I frown. At least with Quantum, communication was job-related. I hope she doesn't continue to chatter.

I round a corner, cross the front of the ancillary portion, and arrive at a point where I can view the gatehouse entrance. It is a singular door, also glass. There is a camera there, as well. I'm counting on my suit to blind that. To render me invisible. The building is constructed like a J. There is the short section where I crouch, the middle entrance section, and a longer section to the east. The ground in the center is paved.

Still no signs of people. I didn't expect many, though. So much is automated today.

Speaking of which…

I detach my remaining monitor and release it into the air. It fires its engine and wings in for a closer look. In the mask, I see its view of the gatehouse. Turns out there isn't one security camera, but two. The obvious one above the door and another tucked into the corner of the J to the east. Suit range should be enough to blank that one too, but I need to be careful.

You are about to do a crazy thing, Radial. Something that violates the mask charter. They want you back, remember? Quantum wants you. Needs you.

I shake my head. No more collections for me. No more.

The monitor concludes there is a standard lock on the front door. It perceives no movement beyond the door in any spectrum. Satisfied, I approach the entrance. I can't help but watch the cameras on the way. The mask tells me that my concealing technology is operational. That there won't be even a flicker of my passage. Things are good.

I use my decoder on the door. It quickly flashes green the door unlocks. I ease it open and enter.

I'm greeted by a long counter with a vidscreen behind it. Reception desk, probably. The counter is empty, and the vidscreen is blank. Again, solace. Comfort. Quiet. Beyond the counter is a transparent wall and a secondary door. This one shows no security, so I swing it open.

I encounter a giant, silver sculpture, teardrop shaped, with an amorphous hollowed-out portion in the center. Not sure what it means. A modern interpretation of bad weather? The halls are light colored, the floor is varnished wood, but dusty. I sense no recent prints, no signs of habitation.

I've entered the right place. The monitor hovers over my right shoulder. With a wave I direct it to my right. It slides up the hall, eventually finding another hall that leads right, back into the short section of the J.

I'm surprised when the wall to its left goes transparent. I spin the monitor for a closer look. On the other side are long beds of dirt. I realize then what this is, with the windows and the dirt. Its a greenhouse of some sort. Now unused.

The entire building seems empty. I'm nowhere near the main complex, though. The reason I'm here is because I've heard this portion connects with it somehow. That I can get there from here.

I'm basing my assumption on a short discussion. A facility employee who mentioned "deliveries in back" then embarrassingly corrected himself. My instincts are rarely wrong, though.

I send the monitor the other way, toward the east end of the building. It finds a hall leading to a garage with landscaping vehicles, and a locked door to the right. I walk down and check that door. It takes three sweeps of the decoder to break it. Inside, I find simple tech storage. Racks of screens and old equipment. Why it was triple locked is beyond me. Historic value?

There are other rooms in the building, both on the main floor and on an upper floor. I search them all without finding anything of interest. Remnants of a paper delivery system, more gardening appliances, broken security devices. There must be a hallway, a connection, somewhere to the rest of the complex. But where?

I return to the teardrop statue. I stare at it, thinking. Should I make a more straightforward assault on the complex? Try to find another way in? Abort the whole mission?

"Do you know why my mother voted me?" Darcy asks.

I shake my head. Communication was a bad idea. With an incon, of all things! A young, possibly spoiled, incon.

"I'm sure there were lots of reasons in *her* mind. Lots of shortcomings. She didn't like my friends, my clothes..." A pause. "She criticized everything. Mostly it was because I reminded her of Dad."

I return to the lake side of the building, then up the hall to the greenhouse. I look at the dirt through the transparent wall. Shake my head. Was her dad blond? Did they have the same laugh?

"We didn't always live in that house, you know. I miss the basement. Almost no one here has basements. But our other house did. It flooded sometimes, but I loved it."

I contemplate taking my mask off. Ending the transmission. But I don't. I said I'd listen. It gives me a connection to what I'm doing. Why I'm here.

I walk into the main hall and turn right past the statue. I find another room that I think was used for security. It is narrow with a long, black desk and mounting screws on the wall. There are wires hanging from holes in the drywall. A layer of dust on the desk.

No chairs, though. Don't security types like to sit? Eat donuts?

"Are you listening, Collector? There's some squirrels playing on the street out here. There's a nut or something. One darts in and pushes it. Then the other. It is funny."

I roll my eyes and keep searching the security room. I walk to the nearest window and look out. Still rainy and grey.

There is another building to the north. It has two stories and is about the size of a typical family home. It has windows facing the lake, but most of them are covered over. There's a handful of people in white uniforms there too. More processing agents like the ones I fought at the North Bend facility. Easy prey for the tranks, but I have a limited supply.

"You know what the basement was really, Collector? A place where I could cry. Whenever Mom and Dad would fight, that's where I'd go. Big tears in the basement."

Tears? Basement?

I walk to the entrance and lay a hand on the transparent inner door. Frown. Just behind me is the sculpture. That odd tear-shaped thing. I take a step back and look at it straight on. Squint.

I pan down. How weird would *that* be?

I adjust the mask's built-in light sensors and do a full sweep of the floor around the statue. I get the image of emptiness beneath it. Openness. Hiddenness. I sweep the statue's surface with infrared and ultraviolet. I find a place in the back that emits differently. I run the decoder over it. It is a switch of some sort. Pushes down.

I work the switch. The statue begins to slide, revealing a square of darkness below it. Complete with a ladder.

The monitor is hovering nearby. I wave at it. It comes swooping in like a trained bird. I point down. It drops into the hole. The space below is a circular tunnel. Lit with tiny blue lights along the ceiling. It appears empty. I bring the monitor back, power it down, and reattach it to its mooring.

I descend the ladder.

CHAPTER 17

The tunnel is remarkably clean and empty. It smells of dampness, but there are no visible signs of water. A miracle in this climate. Constructed to last.

A few of the overhead lights are burned out, suggesting that the tunnel doesn't get much use. Much maintenance. I feel like I'm violating an ancient tomb.

I send the monitor ahead of me, and walk cautiously. The passage has a gentle upward slope. It is also longer than I expected. It takes nearly five minutes to reach the end.

It appears to lead to nothing, though. There is only a grey, nondescript wall.

My stomach sinks. Now what? Should I go back?

I study all three walls. The floor. The ceiling.

Here's where Quantum's guidance would help. Or *anyone's* guidance.

The last light, the one closest to the tunnel's end, is dim and strangely positioned. Too close to the wall. A mere hand's width from it, in fact. Like the hallway used to go farther.

I check that wall again in infrared. Yes, it is giving off more heat.

I lay my hands on the wall surface. Temperature readings

begin to flow to my mask. They indicate a ten-degree difference between the front of my glove and the back. So the wall can't be very thick. Only centimeters.

So do I try to break through? What sort of noise is that going to make? And what's on the other side?

I extract a tiny laser burner from my belt. It is triangular and flat, made to be held between finger and thumb. I depress the firing stud and watch as the violet light arcs out from the front edge. I place it against the wall and see a wisp of smoke followed by a black scorch line. I move the burner back and forth, carving a two-centimeter depression. Back and forth, back and forth. Burning and cutting. After a minute, I feel the burner push free to the other side. I'm through!

I spend a few more minutes widening the hole, then direct the hovering monitor into the notch. There isn't much light on the opposite side, and no movement. Good. I push hard with my shoulder, and I'm rewarded by a crunching sound. I can break this. I brace myself and give it a good hard shove. Portions of the wall's material crack and fall at my feet. Enough that I can now reach a hand in and start tearing it away.

Beyond is a secondary wall. If my suit's temperature readings are to be believed, this one is thinner. I check the light spectrum again. It isn't a wall at all, but a door! The hinges are hidden in the surface to my left. The latch is mechanical, a simple sliding lever. I'm nervous, but I slide it anyway. It clicks free, and I push.

A crack of light shines in, momentarily blinding me. I adjust my mask and move forward. I'm amazed by what I find.

The room is domed, massive, and lit by a single, round skylight. An *oculus*, I think it is called. There is a large double door that leads outside. It has windows, but those have been covered by an opaque material. I'm certain the view was beautiful once. Doubtless of the lake and Green City. Painted along the top of the wall, just below the dome, are remnants of words. A quote of some sort. About having come a long way and grasping for a dream. The words are missing letters, incomplete. Clearly it meant something to someone once.

Dreams and grasping.

The room has lots of shelves around the periphery. There are some paper books, but only a scattered few. The ones that remain are broken or incomplete. This was a library at one time. But now it's empty. Gutted.

Where does the processing take place? Where do the incons go?

I shake my head. Not here. The library has another exit besides the double doors. It leads north to what appears to be a large corridor.

I detect voices. I instinctively crouch and move behind the end of one of the nearest shelves. The sound is coming from the corridor. I slowly make my way around the room's outer wall, headed toward that exit. When I reach the door, I deploy the monitor again. Let it get a quick look.

Turns out, the corridor isn't a corridor at all. It is the landing for a massive stairway that leads up at least three stories. Solid wood and metal construction. Past the stairway on this floor is another room. That door is shut, but it has a single viewing window.

I see no one nearby, so I steer the monitor across the landing to that window. I glimpse long, white tables and men in white moving around. The processing center?

Part of me expected to hear screams. Shouts. Fights between incons and armed guards. But so far, nothing like that.

I enter the room with the staircase and look up. At one time, this must've been a grand part of the house. A fantastically wide flight of stairs. Walls of glass, concrete, and stone. Giant wood beams run along the stairs to support the roof. I estimate the stairway at almost twenty meters from bottom to top. Behind me, there are more obscured windows, floor to ceiling. Another excellent view of the city across the water, I would guess. But that's no longer important. Not to this building. Not to the system.

"It has been awhile, Collector," Darcy says, startling me. "I'm trying not to bother you, but I hope you're all right. Not feeling alone. You're doing what is right. Stay with it!"

I shake my head. Incon encouragement. Nice, but irrelevant.

I'm only here for my friend. Not some crusade.

There's a red flash in my mask—the monitor signaling low energy. I've used it too much. Too many starts and stops. I frown and watch it wing its way to me. I capture and reattach it. It will be little help now. Not until my motion recharges it.

I start to ascend the stairs. Hopefully, I'll gain a better view of the room beyond the doors. It seems like it might. But I feel exposed. The lighting here is bright. Someone in a black collector outfit will make an impression.

As I climb, I watch the wall to my left. It is opaque below, but the farther I go, the less covered it seems. Unfortunately, it is too far away for any close viewing. Not without a monitor. I feel the loss of my second one. I'm almost naked without it.

My calves are beginning to protest. This climb is atypical, even for me. I've counted over forty steps already. There might be a hundred before the end. Midway up, I hear more talking. I hunker down. Someone is coming. From above.

I contemplate retreating to the landing. But that will only make more noise. Draw more attention.

I raise my right arm. My tranker. Better to press on. Deal with these...whoever they are. I freeze in place. Wait.

I hate having the low ground.

Then I see them at the top of the stairs. Two people covered in white. Including their faces. Like inverse shadows of me. They take maybe ten steps before they notice me.

I fire twice. Tranks hit them clean. The only sound they make is when their bodies hit the stairs. There will be some bruising, but I'm okay with that.

I close the distance between us. One of them is slumped against the wall to my right. The other slid headfirst a few steps from where he fell. Both are completely out. Good thing their faces are completely hidden, because I know they're staring at me with a tranked look of shock.

I step past them to the landing above. I find the room they must've exited on the right. It is security locked. No windows. The landing opens up to the left, leading to another door and a room that appears to overlook the processing center.

I grab one of the men by the hands and drag him back up the stairs. There's a camera on the wall ahead of me. It won't see the man while I have him. To the camera, I'm like a ghost. I drag him to the wall beneath the camera, out of sight, and prop him up. I do the same with his twin. Let whoever finds them figure it out.

Time for answers.

I hurry to the left, to the observation room. It isn't even sealed. I slowly open the door. I can hear motion from below, but it is muted. Distant. To my right are three rows of bleachers, thankfully empty. To my left is a glass wall. This is a viewing room, not unlike those I've seen in surgical vids. That notion concerns me. What will I see here?

The glass is slightly misted, indicating a temperature difference between this room and the one below. I feel more anxious now. Where are the incons kept? I don't know what I expected. A big furnace? A molten pit? Some easy way of mass disposal. I crouch and creep slowly to the glass.

I'm unprepared for what I find.

CHAPTER

I have a hard time keeping my last meal down. The image is that striking. There are rows of tables and hanging hooks and a sterile white floor and men in white masks moving, manipulating. I also notice plastic barrels stacked at one end of the room. They seem out of place. Utilitarian.

But none of that is what horrifies me. It is the parts. The disassembled pieces of a human whole. Many humans. They lie on those tables or hang from those hooks. All shapes and sizes, but many smaller, younger parts. More than I would've imagined. It is like a trip to a mannequin store. Except these mannequins were once real. They were animated. Imbued with life.

I think of Jake, and his son. I get this heavy ache in my gut and turn away from the horror. I crouch to the floor and concentrate on not getting sick. Not here. Not in my mask.

I'm struck with how deeply I feel. How *alive* I feel, even in my confusion and horror. What can I do? What *should* I do?

After a few moments, I push myself to my feet. Straighten. I avoid the window. I don't want to look at it.

What are those parts used for? What have I been a part of?

"It is getting really light out here," Darcy says. "Lots of cars going by. I don't think anyone is paying attention to our car. But you know, people get nervous these days."

I have to look further. I have to explore the rest of this facility. To see if there are any "unprocessed" incons I can save. Maybe Jake. Maybe his son. Maybe his ex. Maybe even Lanky Ann.

But how will I do that? All by myself.

I return to the stairway landing. There is more to this complex. Much more, if the rumors are correct. I need to search it out. Aside from the observation room and the one the two men exited, there is a third set of double doors here. It is on an angle between the observation room and the spot where I left the two tranked men. It could lead to other portions of the house. It heads in the general direction of the main drive, so that's promising.

I push through the doors and encounter a wide, gentle ramp that slopes downward. Shallow green carpet, white walls. Typical. I hustle toward the door on the opposite end. Its nearly ten meters away and I feel exposed again.

An alarm begins to sound.

This isn't what I'm used to. I respond to alarms, not cause them.

I sprint to the far door and push it open. Two corridors converge on my position. Here, there is no indication of the house the building once was. Both corridors are painted white with light grey tiles on the floor. There are gurneys lining one, while the other is free of clutter. Extremely clinical.

There are people here too. Both corridors have men in white jackets, doubtless with handheld comm units.

Everyone looks at me. We stand frozen, together, for a full three seconds. Them, because they've never seen someone like me on the inside. Me…I'm simply deciding where to go.

I choose the corridor to the left, the one with the gurneys. I scramble to the first gurney and turn it lengthwise in front of me. It fills most of the hall. A makeshift battering ram.

Some of the men in white jackets duck into the nearest room, others flatten out as best they can. These guys have no training. They're doctors or body disassemblers or whatever. Not soldiers. I push past them. I don't look back to see what they're doing. I don't care. I only need to get by.

I reach the end of the hall and hammer through another double door. Here, there is only a right turn into another hallway similar to the one I left. Another set of doors at the far end. My mask's compass tells me that forward leads east, which is generally the way I want to go.

A phalanx of armed guards enters from other side.

Why am I here?

They're all dressed in green uniforms. All wearing riot helmets. There are five of them. Two hold stunlashes unfurled and ready to go. Two hold rifles, but loosely. The fifth is unarmed.

They're not ready. Not really. Big mistake.

I increase my speed, keeping the gurney in front of me. At about the hall's midpoint I give it a final push, and dive. I fire tranks from both arms, perfectly aimed. Two men drop—the unarmed man, and one of those holding a rifle.

My trankers reload as I hit the ground. *Click-click.*

One of the stunlash men gets the gurney in the side. It strikes the gun of the standing rifleman too, somehow. His rifle goes off, expending a blast of compressed energy into the floor. Miniature lightning traces from that spot outward.

Don't want to get hit by that.

I fire again. I clip stunlash man in the shoulder. Not great aim, but that doesn't matter. He falls backward. That leaves only the guy who fired. He knows he's beaten. He stoops, placing his rifle on the ground. Then he raises both hands. Nice and slow.

I trank him anyway. No time for prisoners.

Ahead, I see daylight. There is a row of windows, and beyond, a driveway. The rain has stopped. There is a counter on the corner to my right. Behind that is the name of the facility. Like these places need a welcome mat. Or a receptionist.

I contemplate the front door. From there I can cross the distance east, regain the woods, and escape with Darcy. Start planning the next step.

But I get a tug, a strong urge. The alarm is still blaring. More men will come.

Quantum is doubtless involved now. Orchestrating. This might be my only chance at a facility.

I glance back and then down the hallway to my right. There is only one door there. Heavy, solid, and locked. I sprint toward it. I bring out the decoder and let it do its thing. I hear running feet. More guards are coming—but if I'm right, if this works out, then maybe they don't matter. The decoder goes green. I push the door open.

Twenty faces look at me. Male and female, of all ages. Not doctors or guards. Incons. They stare at this collector who suddenly broke into their cell.

"Out!" I scream.

Nobody moves.

My external speaker isn't on! I activate it, and repeat the command.

"Out?" a male teenager says. He's dressed casually. Colorful shirt and pants. Like for a day at the local shopping center. "But we just got here. You just brought me."

I'm assuming there are drugs involved. Otherwise, I can see why someone might want to vote him. Dim as a sunless day.

I shake my head. "Not me." I say. "Someone else. Now, out."

An older woman steps forward. "But we're incons now," she says. "We can't go free. The system—"

"You're free," I say. "Now go." I point behind me. "Front door is that way."

The group is stalled. They stand there, looking at me and at each other.

This acceptance of the way things are. How deep it goes. How hard to change.

"There's an alarm," the teenager says.

I nod. "Because of me."

A balding, middle-aged man steps from the crowd. He has a coffee cup in one hand. He searches the faces of the others. "Maybe we should vote," he says. "Vote on whether we stay or go." He raises his cup. "I mean, we have free coffee. Bagels."

The teenager lifts a hand. "That's right, we should vote. All the pozs on staying—"

I touch my mask, engaging the sonic influencer. It emits a high-pitched shriek. Shrill enough that everyone in the room squints and brings hands to their ears. They all start moving past me. Finally.

The teenager leads them to the door. I keep my influencer blaring long enough for the room to clear. The incons reach the hallway, and gather near the reception desk. The path outside is obvious. They should be moving that way, yet they are circling. Dancing like bees around a flower.

I push through them to the front door, then check the halls in both directions. Uniformed guards are storming through the swinging doors. Weapons are up and ready.

From this distance, they won't be accurate. But they can still injure.

I engage the influencer again. The incons start to move. I lay hands on a few, pushing them out the doors and down the front steps. There is a long driveway leading south. If they scattered, many would get free. No one is really moving, though. They're milling around. Some are still inside. They aren't even holding the doors open.

I wrench a door open. A rifle blast penetrates the wall above my head. Energy screams and disperses. I shudder from the nearness. I retreat down the steps. Behind me, I see the guards converging. Some of the incons are around me. "You will die if you stay here," I say. "Your body will be sliced into pieces! Now run!"

Not much happens. The guards reach the reception area. I can't do anything more, except die or be captured.

I stumble down the steps, cross the drive, don't look back. There's a short concrete wall ahead. I scale it.

Beyond are trees and Darcy. I tuck my head, steel myself. Run.

"I think I hear an alarm, Collector," Darcy says in my mask. "Is that you?"

I keep running.

CHAPTER

I reach the SUV and throw open the door. Darcy is in the driver's seat, but she quickly climbs out of the way. She looks at me, worried. I enter the car and get the door shut. Start it. Get us moving.

I hear the hum of drones again. Lots of them.

"What have you been up to, Radial?" Quantum asks in my mask. "I think you've been naughty."

I shake my head. Wish the voice away. I need to focus on our next step, on something significant that can be done. I'm fairly certain that what I just did was meaningless, aside from the information I gleaned. And it might get us caught.

"What happened?" Darcy asks.

The street we're on parallels the east shore of Lake Wash. The car is pointed south, so that's the way I'm going. I drive like a lost soccer mom—slow and steady. On our right is the lake's surface, and crossing it, south of us, is a large ellipse. A drone.

"There's one," I say, nodding. "Can you see any others?"

Darcy looks in all directions. "One way off near Bell's View. Another behind us over the woods."

"Glad I ran fast," I say, but I'm nervous.

We reach an intersection. There are warehouses on both sides. I turn left past a large, blue structure. Ahead is another intersection, and beyond that, a few more blocks should bring us to a freeway entrance.

I hear the hum again. Louder this time. I spot another drone ahead and left, probably the same one that had been over the woods. It is doing a slow sweep of parked cars, of which there are few.

I turn right at the next intersection, and left down an alley between buildings. A green enforcement vehicle speeds by on the street ahead. He doesn't look our direction. I wait five seconds and follow out onto that street. Turn right. Only three more blocks.

Another hum, this time from the right.

"There." Darcy says, pointing.

Past a low, brown building to the south is another drone, hovering. As we draw closer, it moves toward the intersection we'll cross. I glance left. There's another drone there. It is behind us, but a street closer to our position, slowly searching.

They are hemming us in.

"I've adapted to find you, Radial," Quantum says.

I feel a surge of panic and look everywhere for a place to hide. I see only closed warehouses and solitary trees. I resist speeding. Fight it.

Darcy senses my fear. "Maybe they won't see us?" she says. "Because of your suit."

"Maybe." I turn down another side street. A short street. If one of those drones shifts our way, we're history.

I wish I could reach that God that Darcy mentioned. Ask him for help. A blind spot I can count on.

More humming. One of them is moving.

Darcy starts to whimper.

I notice an old mechanic's garage. A remnant from the area's former life. The door is old and sagging. But it is partially open. Wide enough, I think. I head for it, scraping the sides as I pull in. I exit and hurriedly close the garage door.

The humming intensifies until it seems to be right over the building. I hear Darcy muttering. Possibly praying. The humming stays constant. Feels almost deafening. Like it is shaking my bones.

Then silence.

We stay where we are. Ten minutes pass before we drive out again.

***

I don't speak until we're on the highway, until I'm certain there is no pursuit. We blend into the flow of passenger vehicles. I intend to go north, then east, and then south again past the lesser Lake Samm.

Most of what I learned from the facility, I don't want to know. Not really. In fact, I feel worse for the knowing. As for the incons, they're probably on hooks by now. Drained and disassembled.

What's wrong with them? Voting.

Darcy stares out her window. It isn't what I expect from a child. I've heard they are full of questions. But if this one has questions, she keeps most of them inside.

I decide to give her an opportunity. "You're quiet," I say. "I like that."

She looks at me. Shrugs. "You're all I have now. I don't want to make you mad." Her eyes find the window again. "Sorry if I talked too much back there."

"It's okay," I say. "Sometimes you helped."

I merge onto the highway headed east. The morning rush is over. Traffic is fairly light.

"What happened?"

I slowly shake my head. "A lot," I say. "And in some ways, nothing."

"Did you see any incons?"

"Plenty. Some in parts."

Her eyes widen. Her attention focused on me. "Parts?"

I check my rearview mirror. The next car is four or five lengths back. Comfortable. "I don't want to talk about it."

"Oh..."

"I found some captured incons, though. Tried to save them. They stood around like fools. Wanted to vote on whether to run or not...because they had bagels. Couldn't get them to leave."

"So you left them?"

"Had to. I would've been caught." I check the mirror again. Pull into the faster lane. "We couldn't take them with us, anyway." I motion toward the rear seats. "Not in here. Not enough room."

"We could've tried."

I shake my head again. "*They* weren't trying. Why should we?"

The living incons aren't my biggest concern. They're a mystery, but not the one that plagues me most. It is the body parts. The men in white. The barrels. The images still make me ill.

I remember a story, a rumor or an anecdote. People being recycled. Used for food.

Is that what's happening? Is that what we voted for?

"I don't think it is," I say aloud.

"You don't think what is?"

I see the exit for Red West ahead. It is an ultra-tech city. Lots of gamer portals and public comm shops. I need one of those.

CHAPTER

It is a fancy, white brick building—a former bookstore, I think—with the name "Kal's Hot Zone" written above the door in blue letters. There is a lot of glass in front, enough that you can see through to the vintage paper-zine racks the store provides. Those are mostly a prop. A tribute to the way things were. The dates on the magazines are doubtless before Darcy was born. They *do* look slick, though. All these perfectly displayed pictures of smiling, dead luminaries and friendly places. Gives Kal's a special feel.

Darcy begs to go with me. Says she only wants to check the racks. Browse the way things were. Look at actual printed books. That she *loves* hista-pop.

There's danger in that, though. Not from a collector, not at this time of the day. But there are other watchers, other enforcement. Hired snatch and grabs, mostly. A child shouldn't be unsupervised during daylight hours. They always belong *somewhere*, to someone. Either school or parents.

I survey the shop a long time before deciding it is safe enough for her go. The place seems empty. And it isn't where Quantum would expect us to be anyway.

"No peeking on me," I say.

"No problem."

We enter through the front door and Darcy immediately tears off to one of the racks. One featuring teen idols of the aughts. I wind my way through the racks to the information desk on the right-hand side. Behind the angled, wood-simulated counter is a young man, approximately twenty years of age. He's wearing vintage, red spectacles with a white button-down shirt and blue jeans. Over the shirt is an argyle sweater vest. Behind him, the wall is painted a colorful PacNorth panorama, complete with highlighted tourist sites, all jutting out at overblown sizes. The mural wraps around to the otherwise purple wall to my left. That wall has an entrance to the back portion of the shop. Where I need to go.

The tech startles when he sees me. He grabs the edge of the counter and leans into it. A posture of forced casualness.

I'm a mask. I expect a reaction. Even when the timing is twelve hours early. He probably thinks this is his last day.

"I need a booth," I say.

"Uh, sure," he says. "Um, typical rate is, you know…twenty for ten."

I tighten my hands into fists, and slowly release. "I don't have my card with me."

He looks more nervous. "Hey, no problem. We comp collectors."

"Great." I say, nodding. "Which booth?"

He motions toward the wall to my left, his right. Through it, I see rows of black-curtained booths. "Number twelve."

I nod and, with a last check on Darcy, make my way to the booth. The floor beyond is simulated cherrywood. There are booths on both sides. Above each is a white number. Odd numbers on the left, evens on the right. I walk to twelve, enter, and slide the heavy curtain behind me.

There is a soft chair here and a short, wooden desk. A two-meter vid is mounted to the wall, and there's a circular non-haptic controller on the desk. Solid and presumably twitch-free. Nice.

I grab the controller and press the "ultra-private" button. A screen descends behind me, and the image of a quiet park materializes. Birds hop around on the grass; trees gently blow—it's a fairly convincing backdrop. I check the ceiling and find that it is solid sheet construction. No breaks or tears anywhere. The readouts in my mask detect nothing out of the ordinary. No hidden cameras or sensing devices.

I remove my mask, feeling the cool air on my face. How many hours has it been? Eleven? There's a strong scent of cocoa here. Vented in, I think. I remove the upper portion of my suit. Beneath it is the thermal shirt I put on yesterday. It smells a little musty, but it still looks okay.

I activate the vid and look at myself through its built-in eye. After a bit of hair straightening, I'm presentable enough. I sit for a moment and try to recall the number. It was fairly simple, with a few threes and some fives thrown in. I enter my best guess, and wait.

A few seconds later, a message pops up. It confirms that I'm contacting the right person. It is late morning now. The comm system will find her wherever she is. I'm guessing she's at work.

Her image appears. Her hair is different than I remember. Slightly lighter, slightly shorter, and straighter. But still blond. And still beautiful, of course. Behind her, I can see a louvered window and a portion of a white wall. On that wall is a picture of a sunrise—or a sunset—over a calm, purple sea. An oil painting.

Though I haven't shown myself, she smiles. "Radial? Is it really you?"

I work the controller again. Start sending my image. "As you can see."

"Wow," she says. "Great. I thought I…" She straightens herself and smiles softly. "I wondered where you'd been." She glances at another portion of her screen. "I thought you weren't a morning person!"

"I'm not," I say. "But I've been busy." I force a smile. "Work."

Her eyes widen. "I came to your place. Didn't see you. I—"

I grimace. "I worked during the day," I say. "Sorry." I look at my lap, then at the controller I hold. "So how's work? That's where you are, right? The office?"

She glances behind her, then out the window briefly. "Yeah, office day today. Mostly boring stuff. People stuff. We've had a few vote losses. Stuff like that." A quizzical look at me. "Where are you? Looks inviting."

"In a booth," I say. "And the cows?"

"I don't see any…" She raises an eyebrow. "Wait…what?"

"The cows," I say. "At the farms."

"Oh, those cows!" She laughs. "What about them?"

"They're still okay, right? Still producing?"

She laughs again. "You're a strange date, Radial." The smile remains. "That's why you called, right? So we can go out again? Because I would. Or are you using me to get to the cows?"

I find myself blushing. I'm probably way beyond social connections now, with what I've done. But most people—common people—don't know it yet. And they never will, if the system has its way. It will all happen quietly.

Still, it is nice to be wanted. Unusual, but nice.

I feel a twinge of concern. Fear that I might be endangering Heather by contacting her. I should end our conversation. But the facility, the body parts. I need to—

"Radial?"

"Sorry," I say. "Meeting again would be fun." If I wasn't a rogue collector. If I didn't have a child to defend. Or a life purpose to figure out. Why is nothing easy? "Maybe in a couple days, okay? I have things to deal with. I had a friend…go missing."

She gets a look of concern. "Sorry to hear that. Was it a close friend?"

"Close enough. Listen, can we talk about the cows?"

"Seriously?" She gets an odd look. Cautious, but with a twinkle in her eye. "You aren't becoming a skittish cook now, are you? After all that time grilling. The blood, the grease. Does that happen? Overexposure to meat? Meat shock?"

"Now there's a strange question."

I paint on a smile, shake my head. "I'm curious about the

process, is all. You ever seen the cows sent off to market? You know, to be made into steak?"

"Sent to market? No. But that doesn't matter."

"No? Why not?"

She sighs. "Because I've actually seen them processed. Pretty much the whole thing."

I sit back, surprised. "You have? That has to be...sort of...grisly?"

"Not as grisly as you'd expect. Machines do a lot of the work."

"But you've seen the killing? The blood? You've seen them bring in live cows and kill them?"

She reclines and rests her chin on a hand. "Pretty much. It was *real*." She checks another part of her screen. "Life today, you know, is so controlled. Fit into a box of solace and shadow. The butchery, well that was valid and real. Still outside the box."

More to this Heather than meets the eye. "Interesting," I say.

She straightens and smiles. "It is," she says. "Glad you think so."

I hear a knock, and her eyes look away. I hear muffled remarks and watch her face as she takes in what is being said. Her eyes widen slightly, and her mouth does this interesting little...something. A special cuteness. The off-camera voice goes away, and I hear a door shut.

She looks at me again. "Listen, I've got to go." She gives me a gentle—yet wary— smile. "Call me again, okay?"

"Sure." And at that instant I mean it, even though I know I probably can't. In a different life, maybe. A different time. But not now.

She waves, and her image goes black.

I sit for a moment, thinking, watching that blackened image. Then my eyes drift to the other interface elements around it. Digital items, spinning and flashing—begging for my attention. Tiny advertisements and announcements. The kind of things one wouldn't see on a home comm. I already miss my home comm. My comfortable, average, apartment. My old life.

I hear the sound of muffled conversation. It's coming from the inside of my mask! I quickly reassemble myself, and pull my mask over my head. The sensors are alive with activity. I see lots of flashing red. I hate red.

Next comes a series of metallic thumps. Enforcement is nearby.

I need to move.

CHAPTER

I check all the readouts, try to squeeze out any information. Find out why my suit is lit.

"Collector!" Darcy's voice, screaming in my head. She kept the communicator with her. Clever girl!

I wish I could talk back. Find out what's going on.

I scan the booth to make sure I haven't left anything, then stand to leave. The background screen—the smokescreen—is still in place, blocking the exit. With a growl I work the controller, ending ultra-privacy. The screen slowly begins to ascend. I duck under it, grazing my helmet on its trailing edge. I push through and run toward the front of the building.

To my left, the tech is still behind the counter. He looks nervous, white even, but it isn't about me. A portion of the zine racks have been knocked over. Paper-zines are splayed out on the floor in lines, looking like big lumpy tapeworms. I chart the clearest path through and sprint ahead.

Beyond the racks, the store is completely empty. No customers, no Darcy.

I peer out through the glass. I see a man with blue pants and a green slicker. One arm is around Darcy, while the other is working the handle of a black and white sedan. On the vehicle's side is written *Soft Enforcement.* It is what passes for the law during the day. Usually they're security guards who aren't sharp enough to become collectors. In some ways, I'm relieved. I can handle this.

I glance back. The tech is crouched down now, barely visible. "Did you call them?" I yell.

He shrugs. Looks nervous. Typical.

I check my tranks. I still have enough. I crack open the door, then get a series of bright chirps. Impact warning!

I dive to the left as a wave of energy passes through the air where I stood. Somewhere above, in a building near the store, there's a sniper. A fairly good one. Almost got me.

Almost.

I bring out the monitor. Set it loose. Find him!

Another shot is fired at the monitor as it exits. The shot misses, but not by much. My little helper tilts and waffles before righting itself.

Yeah, this guy is good. A collector doing day work?

I direct the monitor first at the soft enforcement guy, whisking his head low enough to make his hair move. He grunts and takes a blind swat. But he isn't that good. Not like his partner.

"Up, up," I whisper, and the monitor complies.

The building on the right offers the best vantage point. The most likely position. I engage the monitor's evade mode. The relayed image begins to bob and weave. The exterior of that building dances by. A symphony of grey.

The enforcement guy notices the monitor's ascent. He stops fiddling with the door and stares. His grip on Darcy remains firm, though. She isn't struggling at all. He might have sedated her. That angers me.

The monitor reaches the top of the building. I get a glimpse of a black roof, and then *blam!* Another shot. The monitor does a complete end-over. I notice a white-clothed head, and then the image is all over the place. I'm seeing sky, pavement, and wall.

I'm worried. Wondering if I should move now, while he's distracted. Not a collector, obviously. Not this early.

The image tips left, corrects, and straightens. I see the roof, complete with spinning venting devices, archaic antennas, and air conditioning units. Crouched between two units is my man. He has a long, dark rifle in both hands, pointed nervously at the sky. The lower half of his face is covered with a white mask, and he has a matching hood over his head. He's focused on the monitor.

Good.

The enforcement officer breaks from his trance and manages to wrench his vehicle door open. He lifts Darcy, shoves her into the front seat. He jumps in, the vehicles external lights snap on, and it begins to back up.

I have to go. Now.

I swing open the door and sprint through. From the monitor's images I see that the shooter notices me. He lowers his gun and takes aim.

I bark an order, putting the monitor in swarm mode. It circles the shooter's head like a deer fly, dipping and swirling. Shooter is occupied.

The enforcement vehicle starts to pull away. It won't be pretty now. I extend the climbing spikes on my suit's forearms and run, hurling myself at the vehicle's roof.

I slip across the surface. I feel my arms drag along the rear window glass, screeching, before digging into the bottom sill. My feet make contact with the pavement. Not good. The car darts forward, turning out of the parking lot into the street proper. Traffic is light, but not absent. I'm now a spectacle—a mask dragged behind a transport. The materials in my boot heels create a shower of sparks. My calves feel the strain.

I lift an arm, try to get a better position.

Blam! The surface of the road near my feet pitches up. I glance toward the store, and simultaneously check the monitor's image. Despite the distraction, the shooter has repositioned himself to fire. I urge the monitor again, ordering it into a tighter circle. The man still manages to shoot.

A sizzle of energy finds the pavement, but this time it helps. I use the momentum to charge forward. I dig into the vehicle's roof. First one arm and then the other.

The store recedes. I recall the monitor, but its image goes black. Out of range!

I feel a twinge of loss, knowing it was my last one. It will obey its final command. It will continue to swarm him. But it is lost to me now.

The vehicle lurches as the driver shifts lanes. My arms hold tight. I'm not giving up.

There's a loud bang, and a hole appears in the roof centimeters from my head. The driver is shooting! Another hole opens up near my right shoulder. Next, I hear the back window blow out. I feel the weight of it collapse beneath me, and the sting of something on my left thigh. I've been hit! The suit deflects, resists puncture, but this hurts. Really hurts.

The loss of the window has given me an opportunity. I disengage my right arm, and prepare to relocate. The car shifts wildly and my entire body leaves the roof. I'm thrown over the left edge, my torso draping the vehicle's side. Only my left arm holds me, and it is screaming with the strain. The vehicle is very nearly in the oncoming lane, I realize. A white delivery truck is headed straight for us. My suit can't stop that.

I hear a scream. Darcy is awake. Must be pounding the driver. Distracting him. The truck hurdles toward us.

The sedan lurches into the right lane. The motion takes me farther over the left side. My feet find the pavement again. More sparks.

No! I flail my right arm, angle it so the spikes point toward the roof, and slam it down.

It digs in. I pull forward, release my left arm, and rip into the roof's surface. I draw myself up and out of the way.

The truck barrels by. I feel the wind of its passing. I take a deep breath, then climb until I'm astride the roof. I straighten myself. Prepare.

I bring my knees up, angle my feet through the shattered rear window, and—releasing my arms—drop inside.

The enforcement officer glances at me, eyes maniacal. He brings his right hand back. It's holding a revolver of some sort. Small, silver, and clearly deadly. Clearly can make some holes. He levels it at my chest. I suck in my breath, brace for the pain.

Darcy's hands reach out. I detect movement of her knee, of her left foot. The officer lets out an *oof* as she finds his stomach. The revolver fires, but I close the distance. I move down and forward. Grab his shoulder. Raise my right arm.

I trank his leg. He yells and then he's out. Comatose.

Darcy's eyes go wide. She glances at me, then at the vehicle's steering wheel. We are listing to the left. Toward oncoming traffic.

I try to reposition, to reach over the bulk of the enforcement officer, but there is something on the floor back here. Lots of things. Hard munitions, wrapping paper from various restaurants, food bags, junk.

I slip. I can't grip the seat, much less throw an arm over. Get to the wheel.

We're in the left lane again. The accelerator seems to be stuck. I lurch up, feel my injured leg hitch against the seat. Grimace. Cry out. Slip back down.

Suddenly the car jerks to the right. Did we hit something?

Darcy has a hand on the wheel. One leg is thrown over the officer's right leg. She's attempting to sit on his lap. Or reach the pedal. Or something.

"No, let me!" I shout. The ride smooths out enough that I can begin to climb over. To help.

"I'm okay," she says.

"No—"

Darcy repositions herself, managing to get both hands on the wheel *and* reach the brake. I watch, aghast, as she stretches up to see where she's going, then scrunches down to manipulate the vehicle. Slowly, persistently, she guides the vehicle to the side of the road and stops.

I check behind us, then push open the door. Darcy found a good place. There's a patch of trees and some smallish buildings along the side of the street here. Quick concealment from anyone on the road.

I open the driver's door and pull Darcy free. I carry her to a spot beneath the trees and briefly search the skies.

I give her a once over. She looks fine. Isn't even crying. "We need to get out of here," I say. "Find a new car."

Darcy crosses her arms. "See," she says. "I told you I could drive."

CHAPTER

I can't help but check the rearview mirror. Again and again I check it. I keep sweeping the road ahead as well. This day isn't even half over, but it has been incredibly long. I find myself driving in circles. Following long streets until they end, until I'm forced to turn. Then I repeat.

Darcy is asleep on the seat next to me. Curled up with her head resting on the passenger door as if she had a bedtime snack and a story. Oblivious. Content. Incredible.

I'm tempted to return to Jake's house. To eat and possibly nap myself. I'm spent.

But I can't. I've stirred things. Saving Darcy, sneaking into the lake facility, the fight with enforcement. Heavy stirring. Those who pursue us are stealthy, and though they probably won't attempt an all-out search until nightfall, I know they are watching. That they will come. With snipers.

Plus, the dog bot at Jake's. I don't know for sure, but I suspect those are supposed to check in from time to time. It wouldn't be wise to go back there. It would be better to find another house for sale. Defeat the dog, raid the fridge, stay a night, move on again.

I worried that my life was a large loop before, but now…?

Eventually, I get tired of driving, of looking, so I meander my way to the lesser lake. I enter one of the woodsier parks that brim it. Wind my way through the parking area until I reach an especially shadowed spot and pull in. I glance at Darcy. Still sleeping.

Why did I let this happen? Save an incon? What was I thinking?

I poke the tear in my suit where the enforcement officer's projectile caught me. There is some pain, but not bad. I'm wounded, but not slowed. Not really. There shouldn't be a bruise. I rarely bruise. Good suit.

Why do I keep wearing my mask? This suit? It would be easier to blend in without it, right? To find places to stay. To hide. To run—

Because it feels safe. Because it fits me. Fits me better than the other life. The life of grilling and interacting. The pressure to hide who I really was. If I'm the mask all the time, I don't have to hide. I'm simply me.

Even in the mask, the me I *was* is not the me I *am*. How to rectify that? How do I go on?

Darcy lifts her head and looks quickly around—startled—then looks at me. Straightens in her seat. "I know this park," she says. "There's a play area over there. They have swings." She looks hopeful. "Can I go?" She points. "It is just over there. See?"

Even here, now, she seeks normalcy. I shake my head. "It isn't a good idea. We shouldn't stay long."

She raises her hands. "No one would know I'm incon, right? I'm just some kid."

I grip the steering wheel. "We're in a stolen car.

She smiles. "Yes, but it's a *new* stolen car." She scans the dash, pats the armrests. "A nice, blue, stolen car. I like blue."

"That doesn't help." I look the direction she pointed. There is a small playground there, with swings and a slide. All green and yellow. Potential lacerations and broken bones. How did *that* not get voted?

She continues to stare at me, her eyes now repeating the question.

Children befuddle me, but I like them. "I don't know what to do next," I say. "We can't go back to Jake's. Can't go to my place."

"What about the person you called?" she says. "You know, at the comm place. Can they help?"

"We're not that close," I say. "Not yet." I pause. "Probably not ever."

She raises one eyebrow. "Was it a girl? A significant?"

I tap my helmet. "I'm a collector."

Darcy frowns. "Mom had lots of significants. Noisy significants. Busy, noisy significants. And smelly."

I chuckle. Smile within my mask.

"We should go to my uncle's. We'd be safe there."

"Your uncle's," I say. "Where is your uncle?"

"See Tee," she says. "Dredge Street"

I straighten with surprise. "See Tee? Who lives in See Tee?" The quadrant used to surround an airport, back when people traveled that way. Before the nation split and the eruptions. Before airplanes got voted for being too dangerous and loud. The name was different then too.

Now See Tee is slums surrounded by abandoned fields. Areas that should've been voted that manage to survive because they serve people's vices. Anonymity is paramount there. No one wants to risk their matrix on a night inside See Tee's shadows. So "no one" does.

"My uncle," she says. "He's kind of special."

I sniff. "He would have to be."

"He is. Different. Says he's vote-free. That they leave him alone. So that's where we should go."

I check the playground. Empty and waiting. "To See Tee?"

She nods her head. Smiles.

I have no better ideas, so I shrug, set my hand on the starter. "Okay, so we'll go to See Tee."

Her smile brightens. "Now that we have that settled…can I go out?"

I stare.

"The swings, remember?"

I settle back into the seat. "Fine. The swings. Four minutes," I say. "I'll watch."

Not napping. Definitely not napping. Only watching.

***

An hour later, we arrive at Darcy's uncle's "house." It isn't a house at all, though. It is a concrete tower that had significance to the airport. Now it juts up from an otherwise empty and overgrown field. The road we approach on is hardly a road. It is heavily cracked and worn, with grass growing through it too.

Trees have reclaimed much of this area, but I can see remnants of civilization in the distance. Wide buildings with finger-like structures. Abandoned airport terminals, I think.

Though rounded at the top, the tower is more square than circular. The only windows are at the apex, and they ring the whole thing. Her uncle has a good view, that's for sure. The top must be at least seven stories up. From here, it is impossible to know if anyone is home.

The building has a square covered entranceway that also appears to be concrete, though it's three shades lighter than the tower. There were two physical glass doors at one time—perhaps an entrance and an exit—but one has been boarded over entirely. The rightmost door has boards instead of glass too, but a handle is apparent. The boards on the leftmost "door" are grey to match the exterior, but the boards in the functioning door are pastel green, orange, and blue. Like a child painted them.

I test the colored door and find it locked. Out of habit, I bring out my decoder and sweep it. The first sweep gets me red, as does the second, and the third.

"That won't work," Darcy says, frowning. "Do you always break into places?"

I shrug. I follow my training. My reality.

She shakes her head. "It's manual," she says.

"Manual?"

"He unlocks it from the inside." She raises her hands.

"There's a camera around here somewhere, I think. A way for him to know we're here."

I scan the exterior. Nothing but solid grey except the lines of mortar between blocks. If there is a camera, it is well hidden. Camouflaged. Maybe inside one of the bricks? "It's probably showing him nothing right now, though," I say.

Darcy looks at me, puzzled. We haven't talked much about my suit. About what it is capable of.

"Invisible to cameras, remember?"

She nods. "He probably wouldn't open for a collector, anyway."

I chuckle. "Probably not." I examine the door again. Only boards and a grey handle. "So, now what?"

Darcy waves her hands above her head. "He should see *me*. Recognize me and let me in."

I inspect the tranking mechanism on my arms, running a hand over each. I've got three tranks per. Six altogether. "Depends on the camera tech," I say. "With older tech, the masking has a wider range. A bigger bubble." I shift my stance. Wish I had a cooking spat to clang together. "It might be blacked out completely."

"So can you back away, then? Go back near the car?"

I move into the high-standing grass until I'm a good five meters away. I nervously scan the horizon. Past an outlying highway, I see small houses and business buildings. Flashing marquees. I feel a bit like a lion in its habitat. A lonely, male lion.

Darcy waves her hands again. Circles. Does an odd little dance. Then she stops and brings a finger to her lips. Looks thoughtful. Next she walks to the door and knocks with both hands. This makes me smile because, if her uncle lives near the top of the tower, there's no way he can hear that. She continues knocking, though.

I continue smiling.

There's a pop and hiss followed by speaker feedback. The sounds are loud enough that I check again to see if anyone heard. I see the same distant dwellings and no motion whatsoever. No one heard.

A male voice cracks over hidden speakers. "Is that you, Darcy? Blink, you've gotten big!"

I try to locate the voice's source, but find nothing obvious. The speakers might look like cement bricks too.

"Uncle Saul?" Darcy says, straightening with excitement. "Yes, it's me!"

"Scales…it has been so long. Is your father with you?"

"No…"

"Well, why are you here? *How* are you here?"

I contemplate moving toward Darcy, if only to show my support. My presence.

She must sense it, though, because she looks my direction and raises a hand. "I have a friend," she says, "who brought me."

There is a long pause. "One of your mother's friends? Because they're not welcome."

Darcy stretches up on her toes. "No, not them." A sigh. "It is strange."

Another pause. "So who's the goon in the grass?"

He can see me? How? I take a cautious step forward.

Darcy looks at me. Shrugs. "That's my friend."

And yet another pause. "Your friend dresses like a collector. Did you know that?"

She looks at me, rolls her eyes. "Yes…"

"So you brought a crazy collector here, without your father…to see me." Silence, and then: "Crazy always goes first, you know." A wild cackle. "The vote! The system! Hurray!"

I feel nervous. He's right about "crazy." Those with mental disorders always become incons. But *he* sounds a bit unsettled now. And if he's crazy, why is he free?

Darcy motions for me. I walk out of the grass to the entranceway. The speakers hiss again, then there's an actual whistle. "Whoo-whee. He has the full outfit. How is that possible? Is it Halloween?"

"Halloween?" Darcy says.

"Old holiday," Saul says. "Got voted. Offended the real witches."

Darcy draws close to the door. "Can you just let us in? He's safe, I promise."

"Hmm…"

"Please?"

"Well…I suppose. I'm very busy today, you see. Lots to fix. Lots of chores. But I could take a minute. A break! Why not!"

Darcy turns to me. "He fixes things."

I nod. Genius and crazy. Sons of the same mother.

The door makes a buzzing sound and snaps free. Darcy pulls it open, and I follow her inside. The interior is darkened, so much that we enter into shadow. The mask amplifies ambient light, thankfully. Gives me the best image possible. Always.

The floor is hard tile, patterned black and white. Dusty. There is clutter everywhere. In the corners, large objects are piled. Vidscreens, wires, mechanical gears. Tubes.

Directly ahead, the room is bisected by a stairway. I'm guessing this place has lots of stairs. Above the stairs are the remains of a long, white, birthday banner. It is tacked up in multiple places so that portions of it are still legible. The message is lost, though. It now says, "Ha Birth y!" There's a pair of wilted balloons up there too. A green one and a red one.

There's a squawk, and a white object appears above the stairway railing. It is humanoid with flashing, red eyes. Then there's a string of popping sounds. The sounds of gunfire.

I dive toward Darcy, and knocking her to the ground, roll back toward the stairway and the object. Blind fire a trank.

The trank connects. The white object hisses and pops, followed by a bright flash of electricity. Next comes a garbled laugh and the beginnings of a song. The birthday song, I think. I climb to my feet, as does Darcy.

"Why did you do that?" she asks.

I shake my head and move slowly toward the stairs and the now-smoking figure. A light comes on above its head, revealing it as a mechanical clown—complete with orange hair and bright painted face. The face is blackened in a few places now, though, and slightly misshapen. A ruined mechanical clown.

"Your uncle is strange," I say.

Near the entrance of the stairs, a vid flickers on. The image of a male face appears. It is painted blue with bright red lips.

"Did you kill Ketch?" The face's eyes flare large and blue. "Oh, man, you killed Ketch!"

I grip Darcy's shoulder. "Is that your uncle?"

She shakes her head. "No, but it's one of his favorite vid aliases. I think he calls it 'Gundy.'"

"Gundy?"

She smiles. "Yeah, isn't it fun?"

"Fun…yes..quite fun."

The image changes to that of an old woman. Pink hair. Silver teeth. "Now you die!"

There's a loud hiss, and a cloud of steam releases from the top of the stairs. Out of that cloud appear a dozen black monitors. They follow the stairs down, flying in a direct line toward us.

These monitors are different from mine. They are faster, sleeker, thinner. Also quieter. They move like a whisper.

They make a low pass over us, and their formation splits in half. Half go to the left above the stairs, the others go right. They bank and turn, circling back for another pass. There is a repeated clicking sound, and the diameter of each monitor appears to expand. As they turn again, I notice an added glimmer on the edge of every monitor. A flash of silver. A blade?

"I think your uncle has changed, Darcy." I collect her into my arms and run for the door. I smash it with my shoulder. It doesn't budge.

The monitors sweep past the bottom of the stairs. Now they reform into a simple V formation. The point of the V turns and aims straight for us. I've never seen a lethal monitor. One designed to injure. I set Darcy down and fire a trank. Miss. I shake my head, aim for the lead monitor, and fire two tranks simultaneously.

Hit! That monitor spins off into the back of the room. I hear it impact the wall.

Doesn't affect the other monitors at all. The formation reforms, and another takes the lead position. I double fire at it, but miss high and low. My tranks are gone.

The vidscreen still shows the old lady. She leans close and

shakes her fingers. "It isn't nice to break people's toys," she says.

I need something to fight with.

I search the floor, the room's corners. I want something that can be thrown or is in some way useful. Something that can protect us. A metal plate we can hide behind.

Finally, I spot an object that makes me smile. In the shadow of a cardboard box—a baseball! I scramble and snatch it up. I fire sidearm at the lead monitor. Hope for the best.

I miss, but the ball manages to wing a monitor on the right side of the formation. It dips and flutters backward into another. A chain of collisions ensue. There is a clatter and a whining, sawing sound. I smell grease and plastic burning. In the end, four monitors flutter from the sky. One lands near the door, another—in pieces—lands beneath the stairway. The third hits a support pillar, bounces all the way down, leaving divots as it goes. It then rolls around on the floor like a pie pan.

The vid image changes. The old lady gapes, mouth wide. She has no teeth. The mouth seems enormous. Like it might swallow a cantaloupe. "That wasn't very nice."

The remaining monitors regroup and circle back toward the stairs. They signal another attack. The blades spin.

"Your suit won't protect you against their blades, collector," the image says. "Two layers of armor material, perhaps. One layer, never."

I'm out of tranks. I have no monitors of my own. Behind me, Darcy cowers in the corner. I search for something more I can use. Find nothing. Only boxes and old junk. Nothing that will stop what is coming.

Darcy's uncle is insane. He's crazy, and he'll kill us both in his madness.

Darcy is against the door, knees pressed to her chest. Her eyes are brimming with tears. After all of it, it has come to this. And this is very, very hard.

The monitors descend, drawing closer and closer. Only one layer of suit. One layer to protect me.

I run to Darcy, throw my whole body around her. Only one layer for me. But to shield her: two.

The whirring of the blades continues. They draw nearer and nearer. I brace for impact. For the inevitable pain. Darcy sobs against my chest. I hold her tighter, say it will be okay.

The whirring stops. I wait a few moments, then glance behind me. The monitors freeze in place. They hover at the bottom of the stairs, then simply angle and follow its incline up. They disappear into the smoke.

I keep hold of Darcy, but she peeks around my left shoulder.

The screen image becomes a stylized cartoon grape with eyes and a mouth. "Now, why would a collector worry about life and death?"

I draw closer to the girl again. Protectively. I can't help it.

"*Why?*" the grape asks. "Why does that happen? Someone should answer, don't you think?" The grape rolls to the right corner of the screen, then to the left. It bounces in place. And we hear laughter.

I exchange looks with Darcy.

She shrugs. "My uncle *is* strange."

"Your uncle is dangerous."

The grape shrinks to half its size and then pops, leaving the screen blank. Dark.

The stairs begin to move slowly upward. They aren't stairs at all. Escalator! Saul's voice fills the room. "You have a bit of a ride ahead of you. I'm at the top."

I take Darcy's hand, and together we enter the escalator. "And we should trust you?" I shout.

A sigh. "Of course, collector. Those blades were dull."

CHAPTER

It is the longest twenty minutes I've ever spent. At each floor, we exit one escalator and circle right to reach another. Every floor is very similar to the bottom floor—dimly lit, with the presence of large storage boxes or stacked mechanicals. The clutter seems to thicken the higher we go. Boxes stacked higher. The amount of dust seems to decline, though, so that's a plus.

The fourth floor is immaculate. The lights are bright, and there's not a single box or pile of junk anywhere. I even wander from our escalator-to-escalator path to look around. The perimeter of the floor has offices. The top portion of every interior wall is transparent. Identical grey trash cans sit outside each office, and every door is open. All have desks and rolling chairs.

"Does anyone use this?" I ask. "It looks like people use this."

Darcy follows close. "I think this is where he tests things."

"Tests what?"

Darcy's eyes search the ceiling. At first, I think she's heard something I've missed, but then she points. I see an object about the size of my hand. Clearly made of metal. Very insect-like. "Maintenance robot," she says.

Another robot, this one long and serpentine, slithers out of one office and into another.

"I think it cleans," she says.

"That cleans?" I say. "I've never seen anything like it. Is it new?"

"Everything uncle Saul makes is new."

I nod, and we drift back to the escalators and resume our journey.

As we near the fifth floor, I detect the smell of popcorn. Memories of baseball games fill my mind. Glimmers of childhood. Sharing a stadium with thousands of fans. A pack of bubble gum in my pocket. Trading cards to be signed. Pounding my hand into a worn mitt.

The outer wall is painted to emulate a stadium panorama. As if we are stepping out onto a concourse. In one direction, I see the ball field and players depicted in action poses. On the opposite end is a string of vendors and spectators interacting. I see a man with a striped hat handing cotton candy to a smiling child. Groups gathered in front of a food counter. Drinks being served.

To our right as we exit—the vendor side—is a row of rectangular machines. One I recognize immediately: a popcorn maker. It is the fish tank variety, with popcorn actively popping inside. It is red in color, and the whole thing travels on three wheels. I can't help but smile as we approach it.

"Popcorn!" Darcy says.

The appliance swivels away from the other machines and rolls toward us. "Would you like some popcorn?" a male voice says. A paper bag drops from a chute on one side. Another chute swings out and dispenses popcorn into the bag.

Darcy gathers the bag and begins eating. "Ooh, I'm sooo hungry."

I'm not hungry, but the smell is hard to ignore.

She holds out a handful. "Don't you want some?"

I shake my head. I would need to remove my mask and I'm still not ready for that.

She shrugs and continues eating.

I hear a two-note chime, and another machine springs to

life. This one is a hot dog vendor. Within its glass is a spinning rotisserie of hot dogs. They are shriveled and brown. Clearly inedible. Doesn't keep it from approaching us, though. "Hot dog, sir? Want a hot dog?"

"I don't think my uncle changes that one much," Darcy says. "I wouldn't eat them."

"I don't plan to."

Another machine lights up. It is blue with "World's Best Chili" painted in yellow on both sides. It makes a sputtering sound before something oozes from the chute. It isn't red. And it is no longer chili.

"We need to go." I take Darcy's hand and lead her away from the remaining vendor-bots. Each one lights up, swivels its body, and attempts to interact with us as we pass. It is disturbing.

The sixth floor is another storage level, though this one is neat and organized. There are bots in service here too. Shifting boxes around, categorizing, cleaning. A large section of the floor is walled off, but there are windows, allowing us to see inside. Within is a large blue construct, dome-shaped. Computational machinery, I would guess. I imagine Quantum looking similar. Except bigger.

"Your uncle uses some math," I say. "Lots of it."

Darcy shrugs. "They voted math at my school. Is it useful?"

As we move to the next escalator, I notice an open flame. A place where something is burning on the otherwise antiseptic white tile. I move closer and realize the "flame" is a projection of some sort. A construct. "What is that?" I say.

The flame reflects in Darcy's eyes. "My Aunt Grace."

"Your aunt?"

"A memorial. Uncle Saul had a name for it. Sounded like 'fire.'"

"A pyre?"

"Yes. That's it!"

"Isn't a pyre something people are actually burned on?"

Darcy shrugs. "Maybe it wasn't that. He said it was made of tiny machines. Experimental. They dance and look like fire. All day. In her honor."

"Machines?" I approach the simulation, hold out my right hand, and check the readings on the arm. There is no heat being generated. Occasionally, there is a streak of purple in the flame, but primarily it is red, orange, and yellow. Maybe some green. Maybe.

I draw still closer and stare into it. Eventually, I detect granularity in the image. It is like standing real close to a vid, but three dimensional. A machine storm built to look like flame. "Like nothing I've ever seen." Suddenly my suit and mask seem really low tech. Backward even.

Uncle Saul must be brilliant. If he can create a display like this, the machines in the lower levels must've been hobbies. Trivial.

A vidscreen flashes to life above the final escalator entrance. On it, the image of a middle-aged man. Shoulder length grey hair combed back neatly. Spectacles— probably of the reading variety—balance on the bridge of his nose. Dark brown eyes.

"Are you coming or not?" he asks. "I have a quota. Time is blue. And choices are dark."

I exchange looks with Darcy. Again, she only shrugs. I check my tranker loads to be certain they're empty. I wish for more.

We enter the final escalator.

CHAPTER

I look up cautiously, nervously, examining every meter of the top floor as it is revealed. It is blue with silver highlights, and it is well lit. Even on this cloudy day, natural light filters in through the windows that circle above us. It is like ascending into heaven.

Soon we're high enough that the entire floor is visible. It resembles a modified studio apartment, with the addition of a lab. Around the perimeter, there are long, curved tables with equipment of every variety. Microscopes and telescopes. Silver equipment, square equipment, flashing and silent equipment.

Saul's personal items are near the escalator. There's a bunk bed positioned lengthwise next to the half-height safety wall. There are cartoon bed coverings on both beds. The top bunk has paper books stacked atop it. Jumbled and sporadic.

Darcy's uncle is behind us, partially hidden by that same wall. He is leaned so only his upper body and head are exposed. He look exactly like his vidscreen image. Mid-forties, though he might be a decade older. Neat grey hair. Glasses. Seemingly well-manicured. Not what I expected, given the condition of the lower floors.

"So here you are," he says. "At last." He gives us an

appraising look, then smiles softly. "Quite the accomplishment," he says. "You. Both here."

Darcy brightens, returning the smile. "Nice to see you, Uncle."

She starts to move toward him, but he raises a hand. "Every journey has a shorter path."

"Uncle?"

A quick smile. "It is easier if I come to you." His head and shoulders rise a few centimeters, then with a lurch, he's lifted far above the wall. For a moment, its like he's being attacked by something from below. Something metal and spider-like. Then I realize that he's riding a construct. He is seated in—strapped into—a mechanical conveyance with four heavily-segmented appendages.

I raise my right arm, but remembering my lack of tranks, I bring it back down.

He leaps nimbly onto the safety wall, and perches there, watching us like a raptor. Noting our reactions. "You really *are* a collector," he says. "The way you move, the way you dance." He scowls. "Not a performer or a well-dressed fraud. But the very real thing. Surprising."

I feel the mask's presence on my face. "Yes," I say.

His metal legs sway slightly, but appear firm. Comfortable. As does he within his harness. I remember hearing that some people—injured people—used to move around in rolling chairs. I've never witnessed one. Never saw anyone immobile, unless I immobilized them. Again, the vote. The system. The loss of people because they were inconvenient to someone. Enough weight in the matrix for Quantum to call me.

"You're surprising too," I say.

Now he smiles. "I suppose you could say that, yes. A cripple, living inside an abandoned control tower." He touches a small control device at his hip, and his spider legs begin to move—delicately—along the top of the wall. After a few steps he turns the corner from the short end to where the wall lengthens and leads toward us. "How have I survived the vote so long, you wonder. Weathered the ides of Quantum?"

I gasp. "Where did you hear that name?"

He waves a hand. "Oh, please, Quantum is no secret. Everyone suspects such an entity exists. Lives revolve around its existence." A smile. "Or should I say *her* existence."

"The voice is female," I say. "You know that too."

He cackles wildly. "I know much about our little game. Our synthetic deity." He glances at Darcy. "That's what Quantum is, you know. A synthetic god we've installed. Another deity to control us. To decide."

He raises both hands. "But this one has no mercy…and no justice. Only consensus." He mimics sadness. "How impure and tragic. Malevolent, yet fair. I'd say it was Darwinian, but it is worse than that. Selection decided by popularity? Nothing *natural* in that." He fans the air. "But it is too late for that discussion now."

He reaches the end of the wall and his contraption gently steps to the floor. When all four legs are clear, it compresses so that his feet—his real feet—are only a few centimeters from the ground. He is only a bit taller than Darcy now.

Saul looks at his niece. "Collectors are trained to be uncaring. Trained not to differentiate. A mocking shadow of blind justice. Given that, how are you with him?"

Darcy shrugs, but says nothing.

He looks at me. "And why are you suited? It isn't evening yet."

She gives me a halfhearted smile. "He never takes it off."

Saul looks at me sideways. "Doesn't take it off? A snake who keeps his skin? How intriguing!" He touches his controller. Immediately two monitors drop from the ceiling and hover near his shoulder. Silver blades extend. "Perhaps we should help him!"

I make a quick scan of my surroundings. Search for possible weapons, possible cover.

"He saved me!" Darcy says. "More than once. And he tried to rescue his friend too."

"Yes, and that's doubly intriguing. A collector who cares, yet can't leave his shell." He looks quickly between us. "Bears investigation, young lady, don't you think? Some sleuthing?" He makes a spinning motion with his right hand. "What goes on beneath the mask?"

He steps closer and points at my chest.

I wave the hand away. "Don't."

He rolls his eyes. "And now the violence. See, that's all they know."

The monitors swoop forward and begin a slow circle over my head. "I thought you said the blades were dull," I say.

He smiles. "Those downstairs are. These aren't. I have to have some protection."

"Please," Darcy begs. "He's okay. He's different."

He smiles at her. "I think we've established that," he says. "But I want to know why! I want to know if he knows himself."

Darcy moves closer to Saul, touches his knees with her hands.

He looks at her. "Don't you want to know what he really looks like? See beneath that mask?"

Darcy shrugs. "He'll show when he's ready."

He waves the monitors away. They return to the ceiling, nestle into a hole like bees. "Well, he must undress occasionally. Collectors have other lives, you know. It is part of their disguise."

Darcy looks at me. Smiles. "Yes, he's a cook, I think. He had vouchers for a steakhouse."

Her uncle's eye light up. "A cook! Wonderful. I get so tired of my own food." He turns and follows a path to the right, leading us to the apartment area. I notice a white refrigeration unit, a stainless steel sink, and a hooded stove.

He pauses in front of the refrigerator. "What sort of cook are you? Italian? Aborigine?"

"Grill cook."

"Grill cook! Excellent!" He opens the refrigerator door. "I have meat!" He starts throwing sealed packages onto a nearby counter. "What is your preference? Top? Porterhouse? T-bone?"

I look at Darcy, then shake my head. "I don't think I can eat meat anymore. Not after what I saw."

Saul frowns and nods. "Yes, the facilities. The logical end to what we've created. One segment living off another."

"So incons are used for food," I say. "As I guessed."

"Chilling thought, isn't it?" He shakes his head. "I don't know for sure. But I suspect. They're used as resources, certainly." He draws his head back. "Why should we let valuable assets go to waste? We live in a closed system. Convenients need eyes, legs…medicine."

I point to the sealed packages. "So these are—"

"Grade-A beef from the farms. I've tested them to be sure."

I study the meat. The SmokeHouse seems forever ago, now. A different life. I'm not even sure I remember what to do. I do get a wave of nostalgia, though. A melancholy which feeds right into a memory of Jake. I lost a friend. I lost a lot.

We've lost a lot.

The system. The vote. The mask.

Darcy places a hand on my arm. "Please, won't you make us something?" Darcy is looking at me now. It is nearly dinnertime. I *could* make something.

I hear a familiar clang and look. In his hands Saul has a pair of cooking spats, not unlike the ones I used to use. He holds them out and smiles.

CHAPTER

With some show, Saul places a fork into his steak, fits a knife between the tines, and draws it back slowly. Back and forth, back and forth. He frees a perfectly rectangular piece—cooked medium rare—and brings it to his lips. He chews slowly, as if testing, savoring. He tips his head back and looks to the sky. Finally, I see his Adam's apple bob and he gives a quick shake of his head.

"Better than satisfactory, my good collector. You've learned your trade well." He takes another bite. Chews a few more times. Smiles. "Both of them."

Seated at the table next to him, Darcy eats quietly. She looks up on occasion, giving me a happy smile, but mostly she eats.

I only watch. Even with the aroma of the meal surrounding me, I'm not hungry. I'm surprised by that. I haven't eaten in some time, but my feeling isn't false. I'm *not* hungry. I don't feel weaker either. Nor more tired.

Probably I'm living on adrenaline. That would be the normal explanation, right? Good genes and good training. The ability to control my urges.

"Have you looked outside lately, Radial?" Quantum whispers. I'm startled by her voice, but not surprised.

In truth, I *have* been looking outside. From my spot at the end of the table I can see through more than half of the encircling windows. I've been checking, watching as the clouds begin to darken. As the hidden sun moves ever westward toward the Olympic Mountains and the sea.

"Are you okay, Collector?" Darcy watches me now. I must've twitched at Quantum's voice. Must've done something to reveal my inner world.

"You've had a day to contemplate your actions," Quantum adds. "Tonight, it is finished. Tonight, you'll be collected."

"Tonight…" I echo, almost whispering.

"What's that?" Saul asks.

"Quantum," I say. "A collector will be sent tonight. To collect me. She's that confident."

He shrugs. "Doubtless she is. Doubtless she knows where you are. She has eyes everywhere."

I'd forgotten how prescient Quantum seems, how all knowing. Of course she watches the city. She would have to. Always well-connected. Nearly ever-present. I've avoided Quantum, but never really escaped.

I remember the zoo. How pretty Heather's smile was. The animals. Even the gorilla. In different times, where would that connection go? How would we progress?

I look north toward the towers of Emerald City. What am I now, really? If I'm not a mask, what am I?

I look at Darcy and her uncle. Both high-value incons. If I turned them in, would Quantum let me go? Let me return to my life? Could I pursue Heather, or a new career, or anything? Could I live?

I get an urge—a wish—to speak with Quantum. To see if things can be worked out. The urge is followed by a wave of fatigue. Not hunger, but a reminder that I am running down. That I'm not unbreakable.

Can I really defend against another collector now? Do I want to?

And what about Jake? And the facility? The body parts. All those incons who wouldn't leave?

What has happened to us? What has PacNorth become?

"Can we make a defense here?" I ask. "Will we be safe?"

Saul takes another bite, smiles, and chews some more. He looks at Darcy and points over her head with his fork, then makes a small semicircle with his hand. "Do you know what this room used to be?" he says. "Back when it was originally constructed. This room. Do you know what it was for?"

"A control tower," I say. "Something to do with the air-field."

"Yes, right, with the airfield. And the planes." He takes another bite. Chews more, and smiles. He studies his plate, and for a moment I think he's done speaking. Then he says: "That's a pretty shirt you have on, Darcy."

I shake my head. All I can see is the ever-darkening clouds. Time slipping by. Meanwhile, I'm here with a lunatic scientist. And a girl. "This was a mistake," I say. "To come here." I stand. "We should go, Darcy." I shake my head again. "Or maybe I should go. Not sure."

Her uncle points upward. "Notice the ceiling? It's black. Painted black. I kept it black."

I hadn't noticed before, but yes, it is black up there. There are cracks and places where lighter colors show through, but mostly it is dark. "So?"

"So!" He harrumphs and makes another cut. Chews. "So, did you see the windows?"

"Yes! What is your point?"

He looks at Darcy. "Has he been like this the whole time?"

I swear and, backing away from the table, stumble into a heavy cabinet. Something on top of it begins to vibrate, and with a crash, hits the floor beside me. I look down. It was a test tube filled with something green. The floor isn't smoking, so I think I'm safe. It doesn't smell bad.

"Tea," Saul says. "A shame to lose it. But only tea."

I look at Darcy. "Has he always been this messy?"

Saul cackles. "The windows are slanted, and the ceiling is black, for one reason. To keep all ambient light out of the way. Any reflected light from vidscreens, or jewelry, or whatever would be thrown upwards to the ceiling."

"Again," I say. "So?"

"To prevent distractions. To prevent misreading." He smiles and chews. "This place was a guide. A technological lighthouse. Men would study screens and look through those windows—" he makes another circling motion—"all the way around. They would control the interaction of all the ships, and make sure they didn't collide. Made sure everyone got where they wanted to go."

I feel like pacing. The sun has nearly set and I need to prepare. I have no tranks left. No monitors…

"Can you replace my monitors?" I ask. "I lost both of them. You have some. I need more. Need to be able to see."

He chuckles again. "Yes, you do."

I growl in disgust. "You're talking around me. Saying things I should understand, but I don't. I'm sorry, I just don't."

His face goes blank, and he watches me. He touches his control pad and his platform rises, backs up, stops, and settles back in again. Then he repeats the procedure, only forward. Still watches me. "Do you believe in God, Collector?" he says, finally.

I look at Darcy, give a hidden frown, and shake my head. "Your family is odd."

"I didn't ask for an observation, Collector. Only an answer."

"What does it matter?"

"Because if you believe in God, you assume a plan. A design. And that's what you're really searching for, aren't you? The design in all this. The plan."

The sky is deep grey now. Somewhere soon, a vid will flash. Somewhere, someone else will suit up. Pull on his mask. Possibly medicate. Then come for me.

"Monitors. Tranks. I need both. Can I have some?"

"We will be safe here. Quantum needs me. And when she decides she doesn't, I have defenses. As you've experienced firsthand." He forces a smile. "We'll be safe…for a time."

Both of their plates are empty. Now no one is hungry. They are still weird, though.

Saul backs away from the table, moves around it toward me, then past me to a narrow pathway on my right. It leads out of the "living" portion of the floor and back into the section with lab tables and equipment. I have no idea if he wants me to follow. Darcy stands, though, and with a shrug goes after him.

So do I.

CHAPTER

The floor is a study in contrasts. On one side of me as I follow Saul is a long mound of his—hopefully clean—underwear. After that comes a table stacked with books, followed by remnants of what appears to be a plastic model project.

On the opposite side, my left, is an empty row of tables. Beyond that, a clear, plastic sheet has been affixed. Within it I can see neatly arranged cylinders, lab equipment, measuring devices, and microscopes. There are vidscreens galore. Most display scrolling text and flashing measurements. Of something.

We reach a doorway that leads into that *clean* area. It is a series of doors, actually. Saul pauses at the first. To his right, standing about waist high, is a brown cardboard box. A rough hole has been cut into the front. He sticks a hand inside and produces a green-colored cloth that he hands to Darcy. "This will be a little big for you, but try it on."

Darcy stretches the garment open, finds the arm and leg holes, and manages to shrug herself into it. Her uncle seals it closed in back. She looks like a child impersonating a doctor. Or a doctor shrunk to child-size.

Saul manipulates himself forward to a separate box—also

open in front—and fishes out a pair of gloves for Darcy. Next comes a full head mask, also green. Then booties.

In the end Darcy is quite comical looking. Like she's researching a disease. Only her eyes are visible through the top portion of the mask. She's smiling, though. "Just like you, Collector," her muffled voice says.

Saul touches a button on his control pad. Instantly a ribbon of cloth is drawn across his feet. The ribbon crosses his body again and again—as if he's a caterpillar building a cocoon. The cocooning stops at his chest. He dons gloves, and another full head mask. He works his control pad and stretches his arms out. The cloth ribbon continues up his chest to his arms and neck. When finished, he looks like a living mummy.

"How do you get that off?" I ask.

"Degradable material," he says. "What I can't rip off will revert to base components within three hours." He gestures with one hand. "There are small mechanicals around here too. They'll eat what's left."

I get the image of small, metal spiders tearing ribbons of cloth from his flesh. The stuff of nightmares.

Saul studies me for a moment. "You'll be fine in that," he says. "After one more step."

He directs Darcy forward. We enter a transparent chamber between doors. I notice a large, slowly-rotating fan above. As soon as the door closes, the fan ramps up, and we're hit with a heavy blast of air. The floor is grated, allowing any loose material to blow away. Following the blast, the fan slows, and the chamber fills with mist. This lingers for about ten seconds before the fan activates again. Another blast, and the mist is pushed into the floor. Ten seconds later, the fan slows to a halt, and the inner door snaps open.

"There we are," Saul says. "All clean now. No lice."

I hear a muffled giggle from Darcy.

We're led to a series of long, grey tables. The one to our left is filled with black equipment. Heavy looking. Solid. Nothing I recognize.

"This is where you store your weapons?" I ask.

He glares at me. "Why would you think that?"

"I asked about new tranks," I say, "new monitors."

"Interesting! I thought you asked about my work." He shrugs. "Well, we're here now."

To our right is a long white pan with a transparent top. Similar to what gardeners might use to start plants in. There's nothing green in these, though. It looks like a thin, fuzzy pastry.

"What is that?" I ask.

"Synthaderm," he says.

"What?"

"Replacement skin," he says. "Synthetic. Grown in a tray for cheap."

I lean closer to the pan and study its contents. I even instruct my mask to enhance the image until individual pores become visible. And the fuzziness? Tiny follicles. Real enough to come from my own arm. Incredible. "How does it work?"

"Work? It's skin!"

"No, I mean, how does it go on? How is it used?"

Saul shifts in his chair, and the chair reacts to the shift. Rising and lowering. Creepy. "Its quite simple, really. Adheres right over the wound." He winks. "Actually, it will adhere to almost anything. Metal, wood, stone, you name it. Adhere and grow."

I don't know what to think. Part of me is repulsed by the idea of skin fused to a rock—or an apple. I'm amazed by the inventiveness, though. The brilliance. "Incredible," I say.

He bows his head. "And with important potential," he says. "No need for an incon's skin, if we can grow something like this, is there? That's the way with many of the so called crises that we rush to solve. If we would only be patient, stay true to our ideals, a better solution would present itself."

He shrugs. "But that's old news." He works the control pad, and his seat moves forward, producing a metallic clinking sound as it goes. He stops at a dark machine that is primarily cylindrical. The cylinder portion is aligned vertically and extends over two meters above the table surface. Its diameter is large enough that I could barely fit my arms around it. There is a rectangular portion that rests on the table, as well. On the far side of the cylinder, is a vidscreen. Saul swings it back so we can view the front surface. It shows lots of motion. Tiny vibrating forms. Pink and green.

"Bugs!" Darcy says.

Saul chuckles. "In a manner of speaking," he says. "Yes, they are!"

I focus on one of the "bugs." There are straight edges. A tiny pinching end. They are clearly machines. "What are they for?"

"Another project," he says. "I call them nanomites. Tiny programmable robots."

"Like the display below?" I ask. "The eternal flame?"

He looks at Darcy. "You showed him that?" he asks. "Told him the meaning?" A head shake. "Well, that's old news too. Should be updated. Those are mindless. Limited functionality." He gestures with his hand. "But these are not. These are cutting edge."

"And the use? Medicinal?"

"The uses are endless! Surgical, certainly. At least at first. But there are many possibilities. I envision a world filled with mite-enabled appliances. The concepts have been talked about for ages. But the difficulty, with the new society, and the losses—"

"Following the breakup?"

"Yes, that. Real research is tenuous. Scattered. Especially in PacNorth. Mites could do many things. Construct, destroy, locate, and find. They could be distributed via multiple means. Your arm appliances, for instance—"

"The tranks?"

"Yes, or perhaps even a monitor. Many possibilities. Very exciting." He looks down, slaps a hand on his chair, and laughs. Even through his mask, it is loud. Almost maniacal. "But again, what does it matter!"

I glance at Darcy. How can such a tranquil child share genes with someone like Saul?

"What does that mean?" I ask.

He grows still and lays a hand on Darcy's head. Shakes it. "Because we are doomed. This society as a whole. Finished."

"You don't think it can be corrected?" I say. "Change the system?"

He shakes his head. “No. I don’t think so. Not without—”

An alarm begins to sound.

Saul laughs again.

CHAPTER

Red lights strobe overhead. They bathe the entire floor with photons that seem to be soaked in wine. Or blood. It is as if I'm standing with two shrouded devils amidst a technological underworld—the microscope, a dark stalactite. Tiny machines of pink and green. Trays of skin. Hellish.

I'm the darkest image in the picture, though. The faceless darkness who surrendered his friends and his life to a system both sublime and sinister. Humane, "fairer than God," yet evil to the core.

"What does it mean?" I ask.

Saul nods toward the ceiling. "An old warning system. Used to prevent in-air collisions." His eyes pan the lab. "Gives the place a interesting feel, doesn't it?"

Darcy grabs his shoulder. "But what does it *mean*, Uncle?"

He looks at me. "It is night."

"This is the end, Radial." Quantum whispers. "So unfortunate."

It feels like my heart got dropped into a fryer. Sizzle and pop. "A collector is coming..."

I expect Saul to start moving, to get ready to *do* something. But he remains where he is, staring at the screen of nanomites. Basking in the light of his perdition.

"How did you know?" I ask. "How could your system possibly know what's coming?"

He repositions his chair to face me. "We talked about plans," he says. "About solutions. Would you like to know what your plan *should* be? What it needs to be?"

"More God talk?"

He chuckles, raising both hands.

"How much warning do you have?" I ask. "How far out is he?"

"Within a hundred meters of the building," Saul says. "Out in the grass somewhere, I suspect." He points toward the windows. "If they're paying attention, they know that we know. Those red lights are clearly visible through the windows."

I grunt in disgust and walk toward the lab opening. Whoever Quantum sent would be the best she could find. More training. More tech. More everything. Uncle Crazy is going to get us all collected. Or killed and then collected. His clowns and vending machines aren't going to save us.

I enter the chamber between doors and almost dance as the fan blasts me. Next comes the mist and the fan again. Is this really necessary when I'm going out?

The outer door clicks open. I exit the chamber and scan the room, the heaps of equipment and boxes. There is lots of cover here. Many dark corners. That, at least, is a help.

I glance at the lab area. Darcy is in the chamber with the fan blowing. Her uncle is still in the lab somewhere. Doubtless playing with his skin or another useless invention. Not helping.

How would I make a collection here? What would I do?

I check the windows that surround the building's upper story. Those expose us. I've never directed a monitor seven stories above the ground, but it is technically feasible. If it were me, I'd already be doing that. Reconnaissance. Searching for weaknesses and the intended targets.

Darcy pulls off her head covering. "What are you going to do, Collector?" she asks. "Can I help?" She looks like she just got out of bed. Her hair is mussed and slightly puffed out—static electricity, I'm guessing.

"Can you get your uncle to arm me?" I glance at the

ceiling. "Or turn on some of his monitors?" Saul is just now entering the vacuum chamber. As the fan comes on, he raises his hands and spins his seat slowly. Like a child caught in a summer rain. "Or at least get him to move faster?"

Darcy strips off her clean room garment, searches briefly for somewhere to set it, then tosses it onto another mound of clothing. "I don't think he's worried," she says.

"He should be. There's a collector out there."

"And there's one in here too, right?" she says, smiling. "So we're even."

I shake my head. "*Even* won't be enough."

Finally, Saul joins us. He removes his hooded mask and makes a few half-hearted tugs at the wrappings on his arms. They tear and begin to unravel. Now he's a sloppy mummy.

"Is there a way to shield the windows?" I ask. "To darken them?"

He smiles. "Afraid of the disk-shaped spies, are you?"

I check the windows again. "And you're not. Clearly." The lights are still strobing red. Annoyingly.

"Never fear, Collector, they will see nothing. Vision through the glass is closed to them."

I point. "But you said they can see the lights outside."

He nods. "Yes, and that's all they'll see. Only the lights."

"A weakness of some sort," I say. "Something you designed?"

He turns and begins *click-clicking* in the other direction. "Not a weakness so much as an enhancement. A preference for that particular shade. An addiction. A blindness."

So he isn't completely mad. Only eccentric. Strange.

"Fine, you've covered the windows," I say. "But the rest? The defenses?"

He pauses. On his right is a collection of chemistry supplies. Beakers, Bunsen burners, test tubes—all distributed across a wooden table. He selects a test tube from a rack and holds it close to his face. Frowns. Brings it to his nose and sniffs. Frowns again.

"The defenses?"

He sighs. "They will be sufficient, collector." He selects

another test tube and pours its contents into the first. The color is hard to determine due to the strobing lights, but whatever it is now, it is about three shades darker than it was. He sniffs the concoction again.

I glance at Darcy. "But we got through them," I say.

He rolls his eyes. "Please, you had my niece with you. That was only a test."

"So they are at full strength now?" I ask. "No testing?"

Saul swirls the test tube. Peers closely. Scowls. "It is best to wait. Gives us time to discuss things."

"We barely have time to prepare."

Saul shrugs, lifts the test tube to his lips, and drinks. He coughs twice and wipes his mouth on his left mummy sleeve. "Shouldn't we at least see what they want?" he asks.

I form my hands into fists. Squeeze them in anger. "Collectors only ever want one thing."

He looks at me. "Yes, you would know that, wouldn't you?"

There is a high-pitched chirp. A single note. Another warning of some sort.

Saul returns the test tube to the rack and moves away. His back is to me.

"What did that sound mean?" I ask, following.

He gives a dismissive wave. "Our company has breached the front door."

CHAPTER

I check the windows again. Could they serve as an escape route? With crampons extended I might be able to reach the ground, but not while holding Darcy. And if I slipped? Even suited, it would be fatal.

"Is there another way out?" I ask. "A hidden exit?"

"There used to be an elevator,"Saul says. "Hasn't worked in years."

"And you never fixed it?"

Saul gives me a look of derision. As if *I'm* the one who's crazy. "I barely use the exit I have! Food is delivered. Supplies are delivered…I don't go out much."

"No kidding," Darcy says.

A humorous remark, but I don't feel it. I can't. We have a large problem. "I need a refill of tranks," I say. "And new monitors."

We reach the dining area. Our dinner plates have been cleared, washed, and are now stacked neatly by the sink. The roaming robots, I assume.

Saul sidles up to the dining table. His seat lowers, and he turns to look at me. "So little faith!" A controlled smile. "Oh, wait, that has been voted away, hasn't it? Faith. The majority got too smart for it. Too distracted. And one by one those that didn't believe voted out those that did. The faithful were holding us back, after all. Standing in the way." He waves a hand. "Efficient system, this voting."

Darcy has a circular, blue toy in her hands. She takes a seat next to her uncle, fully engrossed.

"Voting was a part of our history," I say. "Even before the split. It was called *democracy*, I think."

"Majority rule!" he says, raising a hand.

I nod. "Yes, that's it. That's the term."

He claps his hands, squints as Darcy looks, then leans toward her. "There's another name for it, my dear. Mob rule."

"Mob?" I back away from the table. "We can't discuss this now." I pace left, toward the escalator entrance. Its surface flows like metal rapids toward the dim floor below. Should I set an ambush down there? Or maybe on one of the lower levels?

"Spectacles of turbulence and contention!" Saul yells. He's partially blocked by the kitchen appliances, but I can see one of his hands waving. "Incompatible with personal security!"

Sweat trickles down my cheek. That isn't supposed to happen, but I feel it! Sweat! In my mask! I return to the dining area, stopping where I can see Saul completely.

He leans toward Darcy again. "Short in their lives," he whispers. "Violent in their deaths."

"Is that a quote?" I ask.

"The Federalist Papers. 1787."

Over four hundred years ago. Ancient. Irrelevant.

"Can we watch?" I ask. "You have cameras down there, right? Let's see what's going on."

He smiles. "You're addicted to images. All collectors are. Need more input!" He frowns. "Of course there are cameras. But they hardly seem appropriate now…" Another long look at me. "Or even useful."

I'd forgotten the masking abilities of my suit. The incoming collector would have that ability too, obviously. Yet Saul seemed to see me outside. I growl with frustration. I've never been on this side of it before. I'm not supposed to be. Masks work with each other, not against. Not as enemies!

I visualize a steak being cooked. Grill-marks, flips, and turns. Steady movement toward that time when it is finished and ready to be taken off. Ready to be eaten.

Another alarm chirp. Same volume as before, but about an octave higher.

Saul frowns. Shakes his head.

"What did that mean?" I ask.

"It means they've found a way past the first floor defenses. I'm surprised."

I glare at him, drawing my arms together. Even without my weapons, I could make him help me. Make him arm me. He's older, confined to a chair.

I am none of those things. I'm a mask.

Darcy touches her uncle's still-unraveling arm. "He's good. If we're in trouble, he can help. I've seen it, believe me."

He adjusts his spectacles. Looks at her. "Oh, I know, young lady. I'm quite familiar with this one. His many talents. I've been watching."

"Watching?" Then I remember the computing power in the lower level. The one with the tribute to his wife. "You can get information from Quantum somehow," I say. "Tap her drones, or something."

He nods. "Ah yes, the ubiquitous Quantum." He smiles. "My experiments allow for occasional privileged access. Ingenuity allows for more."

Another realization hits. "Our escape from North Bend. My ease of breaking into Lake Wash. You engineered those somehow?"

He looks at Darcy. Smiles. "I think he's getting it."

Darcy returns the smile.

"But she was taken," I say. "I was shot at."

Saul shrugs, looks at the table, and glides his hands across it. "Well, I can't do everything," he says. "I'm a cripple, after all." He raises a finger. "But I managed to get Darcy collected by the right man, and that was preeminent. After I voted her, of course."

Darcy's eyes widen. "You voted me? How… I thought you loved me."

He touches her head, but she doesn't respond. Only stares at him. "Well, your mother couldn't do it alone, though she was constantly trying. I waited for the right time, the right person, and I acted." He looks at me. "You're not as opaque as you think." He indicates the flashing lights overhead. "Quantum has been watching you too. Gauging your emotions. Testing you. But those same tests gave me what I wanted, Radial. Brought you here."

"Radial?" Darcy says. "That's your name, 'Radial'?" She ponders a moment. Smiles. "I like it."

A metal object, a small glint of silver, races out from beneath a stack of grey pans on my left. It scurries straight for Saul's chair. I bring up my right arm, but he raises a hand. The metal creature pauses at one of the chair's legs then deftly starts to climb it. It is a small oval with legs. A metallic rodent. It reaches Saul's left leg and cuts at the remaining lab-coverings. Diligently works.

I'm reminded of the collector, and the few minutes we have left. "I'm glad I helped," I say. "Glad I brought you Darcy. But there's—"

"A collector, yes. Not very nice of Quantum, is it?"

"What do you have?" I ask. "Weapons I can use."

He sits, trance-like. Staring at me, and through me.

"Uncle?" Darcy says.

Saul grunts. Appears to waken. "You want new monitors. I can give you those." He points to the other side of the escalator and a series of tall shelves. "On the third one," he says. "There's a box."

There isn't a clear path, so I end up shoving three large boxes marked "popcorn" out of the way. After that comes a rolling metal cart filled with playing cards, and a series of what appears to be medieval shields. They move with a heavy clank. Next, I'm stalled by a large covered object—an upright piano. It is on wheels too, but they are small and uneven. Not quite circular. Mostly, I shove it out of the way.

Finally, the shelves are in front of me. Solid black. They

could almost be defined as "organized." There are three shelving units, each with at least six shelves packed with semi-transparent plastic storage bins. Nothing is labeled.

"Where!" I shout. "Which one!"

"Column three, row four."

Column? Row? I step back and find that there is an inherent symmetry to the racks. An equal number of bins in each shelf. Row and columns. Columns and rows. I find what must be the third column and scan up to the fourth shelf. I grab the top of the storage bin and wrench it back. Inside are dozens of circular monitors of different colors and sizes. I shake my head. Will any of these fit my hip unit? "Could you make it easier?"

"Size 32B!" he yells. "They are labeled around the edge."

I lean in and start to rummage, pulling a disk at a time and holding it up to the light.

"In small letters!" he says.

No kidding. I adjust the mask's magnification and continue to look. Finally, I find one that has a "32B" amidst a bunch of other letters and numbers. I read those aloud to be sure.

"That will work," he says. "A bit faster than what you had, but it will fit."

"Does it have blades?"

"No. I apologize. Those aren't designed for your suit. Too large."

Another chirp. Louder and higher. Closer. The mask is closer.

I check the monitor again. It is a shade or two lighter than my suit, but looks good otherwise. I slap it into place. I'm relieved when it nestles comfortably. I get an "operational and charging" notice in my mask. A good start.

I look for another with the same number. Find one that is a dark blue. I don't bother to ask Saul. I simply attach it to my hip. There is a few second pause, but finally I get the "charging" notice there too. I'm a tad less naked.

"And tranks?" I say.

Saul directs me to another box. This one is easier to find, and filled with my size trank. I load both arms. Flex. Glory at how much stronger their presence makes me feel. How much more prepared.

I have to wait out the monitor charging time. Only minutes, but I don't have that. Wish it wasn't that way.

I make my way to the escalator and stare down the well. Should I descend now? Try to surprise them? I check the status of my monitors' charge. Still not there. Close, but not quite. I need all the time. All the functionality. Especially if they are faster. I need to go. The escalator's steps move ever downward. Beckoning.

I take a step, adjust to their movement, and run.

CHAPTER

I descend quickly toward the sixth floor. I look everywhere, scan everything. I see the pyre used to commemorate Darcy's aunt, still flickering and dancing. By leaning forward, I can glimpse the large calculating machine below, its huge dome ever-thinking. Processing. Providing whatever data Saul requires.

There isn't much else to the floor. Mostly it is wide open spaces. Amazing given how packed it is upstairs. Maybe it keeps the floor cooler? Helps the blue calculator? Machines prefer the cold, I've heard. Regardless, it makes the room more predictable. Easier to secure, but also dangerous.

I crouch at the bottom of the escalator and have another look around. I see nothing unusual. I utilize the mask's audio enhancement capabilities and hear nothing there either. Not even the scurry of a mouse—metal or otherwise.

I circle to the down escalator. Wait.

Below is the floor dedicated to baseball. The fifth floor. That means I'll encounter the vendor bots again. Should've asked Saul if there was a way to shut those off! Still, if they detect our intruder, try to interact with him…

My left monitor says it is fully charged. Should I release it now? Let it look around? I try to calculate how far my nemesis could've come. We had three chimes, right? That would mean three floors. I haven't been down here long, but the collector might already be at floor five.

I enter the escalator, but I don't sprint. I crouch. Hide myself between the silver escalator walls.

This is strange. Unlike anything I've encountered since training. No incon ever has skills. Or the equipment. Most are sheep. Blind disciples of the system.

I hate the exposure of the escalator. Plus, while I'm traveling down, the other collector might be traveling up. I resist raising my head and looking over to the up side. But I want to.

The monitor. I need to use it.

The right monitor tells me it is ready.

I smile. Just in time.

I detach the monitors and set them free. They drop and adjust themselves, hover above the moving surface. Within the mask, both images snap to life, forming a bifocal of the escalator in front of me. With a hand motion and a dart of my eye, I send them higher, up near the ceiling of the fifth floor. I have a bird's eye view—a predator's view.

I'm amazed by how clean the ceiling is. Not a single cobweb. The serpentine cleaning bots must be able to climb walls too. Wish we'd had some of those at the Smoke House. Would've saved me a lot of grease baths.

On my left is the side painted to look like a concourse. The vendors have formed a single line there again. They are darkened, waiting. I won't go that way.

I swivel one monitor to look first at me and then at the up escalator. Empty. A river of blind motion.

The collector hasn't passed me. Not yet. Darcy and Saul are safe above. Still free.

My escalator reaches the bottom. I remain crouched and step free. I hide in its shadow, focusing on all the monitors reveal: the murals depicting the baseball stadium, the vendor bots, the rows of stadium seats. I notice a slender robot creeping between a row. Doubtless performing some maintenance chore.

Between the vendor side and the stadium side is a central walled-off section. An interior room of some sort. There are drink machines around it. There are also support columns throughout the floor. All could provide cover. Places to hide.

Nothing seems unusual, though. Not *more* unusual, anyway. The lights feel dimmer, but sometimes it is hard to tell. The mask amplifies ambient light to give me the best image possible. Consequently, the scene is changed, distorted. I'm never quite sure what the naked eye would see. Never sure what is real.

I stand and walk toward the down escalator. Next floor. He must be lower.

One of my monitor images fuzzes slightly. I look up to where the monitor travels, a few meters above my head.

I get a warning in my mask. A flash of heuristic recognition. I duck to the left and a dark object slices by my right arm. It doesn't have the trademark whistle of a trank. The sound is too low. Larger and deadlier.

This one is good. Knows how to hide. Let's his equipment do the work.

I throw myself to the floor and roll back toward the cover of the escalator. At the same time, I instruct my monitors to make wider circles. To search, to find my attacker.

I'm trained too, right? I know how to dance. How to rally. I'm a mask.

I need to draw him out. Uncover his location. Where is he?

The same monitor fuzzes again. I search the ceiling. Try to find it. I call it to me. I see it curve out over the room, a small circular shadow. It heads my direction. The monitor looks strange, though. Misshapen. Larger.

There's something on its back!

The image continues to fuzz. The monitor gives an injured whine then splits into a dozen jagged pieces. They shower the ground in front of me. I'm shocked. Hurt. Sure, it was only a monitor, but its destruction seemed…evil.

What tech does he have?

To my right is the side with the ball field mural and the stadium seats. I sprint toward them and dive into the nearest aisle. Ahead, is a large support column. I scramble behind it. Try to regain my composure.

"You noticed now, haven't you?" Quantum whispers. "You aren't alone." She seems to be smiling. Impossible for an artificial intelligence, I know, but there it is. "I'm speaking to your collector, as well," she adds. "How delightfully surreal."

Need to keep moving. Focus. Bring the other monitor into play.

It answers my call, dropping from the ceiling and making a fast circle of the floor. Eyes out. Looking everywhere. Finding?

I see a shadow on the vendor side. A low darkness hunched between two free-standing drink machines. Near the central room.

I have him.

I crawl to the next section of seats in his direction. I use their cover to reach the next aisle, and then the next section.

I recall a game from my childhood, one where a baseball was hit my direction. My brother and I scrambled after it, but it eluded our mitts. The thunk as it collided with the back of a seat, followed by a series of hollow thunks as it made its way to the floor. My brother cursed. We hit the floor, crawled around, looking. There were traces of peanut shells—back before peanuts got voted—used gum, abandoned plastic cups. Traces of soft drink and beer. Paper cotton candy holders…

My remaining monitor begins to lose power. I resist the urge to shout. I send a recall and hold my position. Increase its speed.

The monitor is behind me now. Ducking and weaving. Following my instructions. I turn to watch.

There is a smaller shadow behind it. The same sort of mechanism that shredded my first monitor, I assume. Another predator.

I lift my right arm over the row of seats. Try to focus. It is difficult to aim at such a small object. Worse than trying to hit Saul's razor monitors. This one is skeletal in comparison. Like a flying crescent with arms. A sickle.

Frightening.

My monitor bobs to the right. I focus. Shoot. Pray.

The trank nicks the sickle's side. It spins, veers toward the escalators, seems to correct, but then flips over and drops into the section of seats an aisle away. There is a screech of electrical misfire, a staccato of heavy clacks, and a puff of smoke.

My monitor flies past me and makes a slow circle. I hesitate, but then recall it. It drops to hover near my right shoulder. I grab it and snap it into place. See the charging message again. It is safe for now.

The collector's last position is closer now. Around a corner of the interior room. Peering over the seatbacks, I see the reflected light of the drink machines on the tiled floor. The wall he is on is still obscured, but I know where he is. I think.

I check my tranks. I have over a dozen, but they aren't as useful in this case. Not against dark armor like mine. I'll need a lot.

The back of the seat I'm shielded behind explodes, covering me with shards of blue plastic. I retreat, crawling back toward the escalators. Away from the room. Seatbacks explode one after another. Hard trank after hard trank. He's loaded to the hilt. Doesn't care if he wastes them.

I reach another support column, then straighten and huddle behind it. The interior room would be between us, *if* he's still where he was. But he isn't. He couldn't be—not and make those shots.

I doubt everything now.

My mask detects movement. A sinewy shadow overhead. Another sickle? Too bad my suit's camera shielding doesn't work on monitors. But of course, it couldn't. The monitors are our eyes and ears. The tranks, our fists.

Fine, let him see me. When faced with a gun, the best choice is to get to the shooter. To get close.

I know he's over by the vendors somewhere. Either back where he started, or behind one of the support columns there. The quickest route is across the open floor between the escalators and the room.

Time to make this personal.

CHAPTER

Monitors aren't supposed to attack. They spy, they listen, they distract.

His attack, though, and they make Saul's bladed models look quaint. They grasp, rend, and destroy.

I detect movement again, then see my adversary's sickle in the sky to my right. It is silent, but I can sense its weight as it swoops toward me. Like it has a thousand pounds of deadly menace. Sharp and lethal.

I dive between the up escalator walls. The sickle skims my right shoulder, then flips, doubles back, and deftly drops onto my helmet. Another new trick!

I hear a buzz saw firing and beginning to spin. It is between my ears in the back of my head. It freaks me. Blinds me with terror. My mask registers the presence; the wound of an incision being made.

I'm panicked now. I stand and stagger while clawing at my attacker. I manage to grab it with my right hand, but an electric shock breaks my grip. I scream, struggle, thrash my head. Any-thing to free myself.

I hear the muddled voice of Darcy, asking if I'm okay.

My eye is off the ball. The real pitcher is still huddled in the shadows, waiting to throw his fastball. Waiting with tranks. I have to get to cover. I stagger toward the silent vendor bots. They are ten meters away, but there is a support column closer. I contemplate slamming my head into the column, but the sickle's position makes it difficult. The thing knew exactly where to grip me.

Warnings flash everywhere. The mask screams lists of danger. The ravages of the monitor's saw. The progress it has made against a projectile-proof mask. A breech is eminent.

I clutch the sickle again and feel the sharp otherworldliness of its form. I get another shock, but I grit my teeth against it. My fingers search for the point of connection. The tiny, barbed feet.

A trank hits my stomach. The wind leaves me and I'm bowled over. Knocked to the floor. I somehow retain my grip on the sickle. I'm still trying to break free.

Through the fog of safety warnings, I see a new shadow. *My* collector. My mirror image. He stands right in front of me. Watching. Waiting.

The sickle is deeply connected. I can't break it free. There is only one option. I raise my left arm. Align it as best I can. Not at the collector. At my own head.

I fire.

There is a *thonk*, and I see stars. My vision blurs. Did I miss? I reach for the sickle. It is still there.

...no, wait. It is attached, but there's no shock. No resistance. No warnings either. I seize it, rock it back and forth, then tear it away.

My vision clears. I throw the monitor at my twin. He easily steps clear. I look at him, try to focus, raise my other hand.

A trank catches my left side. It doesn't break the suit, doesn't touch skin, but it aches something awful. My left arm is numb. I can't retaliate.

The collector draws near. I detect subtle differences in his suit. A lighter look. The suggestion of nimbleness. An upgraded model? Probably lighter *and* faster. Like the sickle monitors.

"We have you now, Radial," Quantum whispers. "And it was disappointingly easy."

I shake my head.

"Oh, yes. First you, and then Saul and the girl. You'll all make interesting studies. Useful resources."

"When we're dismembered?" I say. "Used for food?"

There is a burst of broken static. The mimicry of a laugh?

The collector shakes his head. Raises an arm.

I surge to my feet, firing from my right trank. I miss, but I manage to close the distance between us. Manage to get inside his range. My right fist finds the chin of his mask. I follow that with a hard left to his chest.

The collector cartwheels out of the way. He regains his feet, shakes his head, and unloads on me.

Pain spikes me everywhere. Legs, arms, chest, and head. I attempt to return his fire, but I can't focus. Most of my shots go wide. Then my right trank takes a hit and seems to jam. Won't fire at all.

He uses my misfortune to make it personal. He gives me a hard kick and sends me into the support pole. I wrack my spine and crumble, ending in a heap on the floor.

I bring my hands to my face. I can feel a place where the mask is torn. My temple exposed to the air.

The collector moves closer, right arm still raised. There is a gash in the arm of his suit. A place where skin is visible. It reminds me of something, but I'm not sure what.

"You have received incon status, Radial," Quantum says. "Prepare to be collected."

The collector pauses and his head cocks questioningly. As if something surprised him.

I notice the vendor bots behind him.

There is static and another voice breaks into my thoughts. Darcy's voice. "Are you okay, Radial? Please be okay. You're special. You can make a difference. You saved me. You're good!"

"Popcorn!" I say.

The popcorn vendor chimes to life. The collector's head turns slightly. It is enough.

I kip to my feet, dive toward him—and catching his right foot—pull.

He struggles, but I hang on with all I've got. I'm rewarded when he hits the floor. He's lighter than I expected. Strong, wiry, but light.

There is a grunt and he kicks at my hand. Frees himself. He tries to scramble away, but I dive for him again. Catch an ankle, then a leg. I have—

He swings his free leg and manages to clip my head. That hurts. Badly. I see stars, and my mask fuzzes up. Now I'm beyond angry. Unsettled. Raging inside.

He tries to get to his feet, but I restrain him. Raise a fist. Punch a leg. Raise another fist. Hit his stomach. Hit, hit, hit. Once for each trank I took. Once for all the collections I've made. This guy is going to take it all. The full order of my pain.

After a series of grunts and weak attempts to break free, he stops moving completely.

I grab his left wrist and strip the remaining trank cartridges from his firing mechanism. He still had five. I take the right wrist in my hand and do the same. I make a visual check of the monitor clips at his hips to be certain they're empty. No more surprises. No more weapons.

No comments from Quantum either. She has to know what has happened. Has to read her collector's vitals and know he's inactive.

Despite my pain, I smile. I've won one. This one. Against an agent of the system. I get this impulse, this notion, that I need to say something to Quantum. To let her know where we stand.

I crawl towards the collector's head and turn it so I can see the place where the mask closes in back. I work the switch, split the mask, push it up.

He's wearing a hair net of some sort. An internal wrap—also black—to keep the hair flat and together. Odd. I assumed all collectors had short hair like mine. Blind assumption. I pull his mask to the top of his head where the hairnet ends. His hair is blond.

I get a flood of emotion when I see the internals of the mask. Full connection to Quantum is right there for the taking. There's a mixture of joy and sadness.

The collector's head falls into my lap. I glance at it, startle, then swivel around to get a better view. A flash of memory. My trip to the zoo, the lion cage.

"The females do all the hunting," she says.

And then, as now, it is Heather.

CHAPTER

I study Heather's face for a long moment. Emotions surge through me. They fluctuate and merge, becoming this uneven mix, barely discernible. What do I feel? Shock? Anger? Horror? Maybe all three.

She's a collector. One of the best. And Quantum sent *her* to collect me. To take Saul, Darcy, and I to a facility somewhere. To turn us into "resources."

"What have you done, Radial?" Quantum asks. "Is she dead?" The mockery of laughter returns, echoing over and over.

I wrench my mask from my head and throw it down. I hear Quantum's laughter in Heather's mask too, so I snatch that one up, and with aching arms, toss it as far as I can. It lands near the vendor bots. All of them snap to life.

"Would you like some popcorn?"

"Hot dog, sir. Would you like a hot dog?"

"Chili?"

I scowl and look at Heather again. Did she know she was hunting me? She seemed to hesitate. Did she know? Or was it all Quantum's game? Manipulation of innocents.

Heather's not innocent, though. She's a trained killer. I

think of the facility, and the vote. Maybe we all are. All of PacNorth. *Trained* killers.

I feel the air on my face. Just as it is exposed, so is my intent. I'm revealed for what I truly am. I rarely saw actual death. The cleanup was left for others. The mess! But I was a killer, all the same. If it weren't for my sudden break of clarity, Darcy would be nothing but parts within the North Bend facility. Being studied and processed.

I push a stray hair from Heather's eyes. Such a pretty killer. I see no obvious indication of life. Is she dead? Did I—?

I hold my hand in front of her nose for a temperature reading, but that gives me nothing. My mask is still on the ground! I swear, and reaching for the mask, hold its front surface near her face. It fogs slightly.

She's alive and breathing. Now what?

I hear Darcy's voice in my mask, so I pull it back on.

"Are you okay, Radial?"

"I don't know," I say. "I guess."

"Where are you? Are you hurt?"

"Don't worry," I say. "I'm coming up." With a grunt I push myself to a standing position. I do hurt. Everything hurts. I think I'm finally bruised. A lot.

I stoop and get one arm under Heather, then the other, cradling her. I wish she wasn't wearing the suit. Makes her heavier. Hurts more.

I slowly make my way to the escalator, and propping against the left side, start the ride up. I look over at Heather's discarded mask and the vending machines still trying to sell it something. Their power and purpose restored.

But is mine? What is my purpose now? What do I do? Where do I go?

^^^

Darcy waits near the escalator exit on the top floor. Her hands are clenched in front of her, and there's a wide-eyed look on her face. "It's a girl," she says. "The collector is a girl."

There's a long table to the left, covered with books. I stumble toward it. "Help me." I lay an elbow into the nearest clump of books and push them to the floor. Darcy joins me in clearing, though with a bit more grace, taking a few books at a time and forming little stacks nearby. Soon, the table is free enough to place Heather on it. I release her weight and exhale.

The normal lighting is back—no flashing red. I'm glad for that.

I hear a familiar clicking sound to my right and turn.

Saul stands near the bunk bed, a pensive look on his face. "You've achieved the improbable," he says. "This won't end well."

I clench my fists. "You're welcome."

Darcy moves closer to me, and reaching up, touches my exposed temple. "Can you take your mask off now? I can see your skin."

I shake my head. "You know my name," I say. "That's enough for now." I look at Heather again. She's pale and lifeless. *Beautiful*, but only in an academic way now. I feel incredibly cold inside. Detached.

"Radial Crane," Darcy says. "I still like that name." She looks at Heather too. "Are there many girls?"

I shrug. "I don't know. We never know the others."

"So you didn't know her?" Saul says.

"I did," I say. "We…dated once. But I didn't know she was…this."

Both are silent. Watching me.

I keep staring at Heather's face, trying to remember what it was like to hope. To care about the idea of caring. But now I want a simple end to it all. But I can find no solution. The system is everywhere. Controls everything.

I nod at Heather. "We should tie her," I say. "In case, she wakes up."

Saul moves closer. "She's alive then? You didn't end her?" He click-clacks to the table. "I'm no doctor, but I can check—"

"Tie first," I say. "Then check."

Saul directs Darcy through the maze of boxes to one filled with wires and cables. We scavenge enough to secure Heather to the table. Her body is now criss-crossed with multi-colored cords, like she's being held in place by a rainbow.

"Where's her mask?" Saul asks. When I tell him where I left it, he scowls. "We could've simply checked the biometrics…" He shakes his head. "Collectors. Always making things worse."

Another search produces a handheld computer that Saul somehow syncs with Heather's suit. After a moment of pensive staring, and lots of sighs, he looks at me. "She's badly beaten. Her vitals are weak. I'm not sure…" He adjusts his seat higher. "Do you think she'd have a change of heart, now that she's exposed?"

"I've no idea. She may, but I doubt it." I recall the time I called her from the bookstore. Right before we were attacked. "She said she liked to watch cows being butchered. That it was real."

Saul brings a hand to his chin, thinks for a moment. "Perhaps we should leave her tied."

I notice the kitchen area. I'm hungry again. Famished.

"Will another collector come?" Darcy asks.

I shake my head. "Not tonight. But soft enforcement might try in the morning. And that night, another mask."

Saul scowls. "Not very nice of Quantum, is it? Sending collectors here until we're taken. She's single-minded in her pursuits. Persistent."

Exhaustion starts to set in. My arms feel ready to fall off. "We can't stay here," I say. "We have to move."

Saul makes a clucking sound. "You still want to play little ball, Radial," he says. "Bunts and base hits. Running and cowering. But it is time for a new strategy."

"What's that?" I say.

"A home run."

CHAPTER

It isn't the time for baseball references. I'm in a locked room with an old man and a little girl, and more wolves will come. Even if we replenish Saul's defenses, even if they hold up for another night, they won't last forever. Quantum *is* persistent, and she *always* takes the long view.

Wish individual voters would do the same.

"What are you suggesting, Saul? What do you want me to do?"

His ribbons of lab covering are gone now. Eaten by the metal mice. "We have an opportunity," he says. "With you. Not only to change the system, but to break it."

"And how do we do that?"

He adjusts his seat then rests his chin in his hand. "Attack the source, of course."

"The source? You mean the voters? Manipulate VoteMAX somehow?"

He cackles. "The voters aren't the source. Merely accomplices. Both willing and unwitting." He points to the side of his head. "The source is your digital mother."

A weight settles on my shoulders. Like I got buried by one of the mountains. "You want *me* to take on Quantum? Impossible."

"You defeated one of her best. That was impossible."

I glance at Heather. I barely stopped her. Barely. And what sort of defenses would Quantum have?

I shake my head. "No one even knows where Quantum is. She could be distributed throughout the city for all I know. Redundantly copied. Everywhere."

"She isn't," he says. "And you know it. She's a synthetic brain—"

"Hidden somewhere in the city." I find it hard to be near Heather. I pace away from her table until I'm stopped by a box with a large artificial palm tree sticking out of it. There are metal bugs tied to its branches. "I know her description. All collectors know it."

"It is her biggest weakness," Saul says. "And I know where she is."

I glare at him. "Then why don't *you* take her out?"

He indicates his spider harness and his legs. "I don't have what it takes—in many ways." He points at Darcy. "You saved Darcy. You've proven your worth. But the only way to permanently guarantee her safety, to guarantee *anyone's* safety, is to do something revolutionary."

I have trepidations. Fears. But if I had my vote, I'd rather be attacking than defending. Collectors aren't made to defend. That's for soft enforcement.

I remember Quantum's laughter. The shock of knowing she'd pitted Heather against me. If I'm a trained killer, then there's only one thing I'd like to kill now. I hate the idea, but I also love it. "Fine," I say. "I'll do it."

Saul nods slowly. "Then I should warn you, Radial Crane, that this will unmake you. Like the Garden. The apple. Unmake you."

I look at Darcy. "What is he talking about?"

Saul shakes his head. "You can't be so lost, can you?"

"Lost," I say. "Yes, I supposed I am. The apple?"

He sighs. "Creation story. Man and woman in a garden. God says they can have anything to eat except from one tree—the Tree of the Knowledge of Good and Evil. They are tempted, they fail, they eat."

Air passes across my temple. It feels incredibly strange now. Fresh air. I've been so long in the suit. "And so?" I say. "Then what?"

"They are changed. Their world is changed. Whatever they were before is lost forever."

"They were punished, right?" Darcy says. "They were kicked out."

Saul nods. "Yes, but the change is not a punishment. The change is merely a result of their actions. Of their eating."

Heather moans and her head shifts, but she remains unconscious. Eyes shut.

"Change is necessary here," I say. "Change is needed."

Saul works his controls. Raises and lowers his seat. A nervous adjustment. "I think it is inevitable." A smile. "I only wanted to be clear. To warn you." A pause. "You're certain?"

I give a slow nod.

"Then you'll need more upgrades. And repair…" He looks at the ceiling and the encircling windows. "And some upgrades. "

"You've said that already, uncle."

He gives Darcy a confused look.

"The upgrade part," she says. "You said that."

"Yes. He'll need some." He frowns at me. "I don't suppose you want a plan too. Because I'm not as qualified with those." He scans the heaps of books and the nearby kitchen area. "So, attack at dawn? That seems appropriate, doesn't it? After your kind have gone to bed?"

"I suppose so, yes."

"Very well," he says. "Let's change things." His voice lowers and there's the hint of a frown. "If we can."

***

The remaining hours of darkness are irregular. My tranks and monitors are replaced, my mask and suit are repaired and augmented. I even manage to sleep some.

I awake often, every time hearing the Saul's ruminations

from somewhere on the floor. Once, I see him open the refrigeration unit—its internal light glowing like a beacon in the center of the room. Once, I hear him fuming out loud, arguing with unseen assistants. And once I'm sure he's checking on Heather. Possibly talking to her. Or arguing with her.

Another time, all he does is laugh. That disturbs me the most. His laugh is not a happy thing. It is the sound of a man who has reached the darkest cavern of his mind and now struggles for the light. The sort of place that in different times would find him locked within a padded room.

Darcy slept the whole night on a small cot that her uncle found. She rested, turned on her side, with a tiny smile on her face. A face that should be able to live forever, smiling. Without threat of a vote or of becoming inconvenient.

That is what drives me now. To end it. To break the system.

I will end Quantum. I am the Mask.

Saul did what he promised. I'm to a place where I feel right again. Ready. There are both soft and hard tranks in my possession. My launcher is full. My new monitors have blades of their own. More speed. My visual connection to them is perfect. He even finds a way, he thinks, to make me momentarily disappear from opposing monitors. If that works, that will be a decided advantage. The suit's blurring effect times two.

Now I lean against the escalator, mentally preparing myself. My eyes linger on the view through the windows to the east. It is a clear morning. An unusual morning. The distant Cascade Mountains are visible—gray and purple shadows before an oncoming sun. I suppose it would be seen as beautiful, majestic. Poetic even. But I'm no judge of art.

I hear Saul's click-click behind me and turn. Darcy is with him. Her hair is mussed, but there's a smile on her face.

In his hands are two objects. One is long and narrow—a modified trank of some sort—the other is a small, round disk. "Two things you'll need." He holds up the disk and motions me closer. "This attaches below the chin of your mask. It is for communication with us." He smiles. "Both ways."

I nod.

"You'll lose all contact with Quantum. Are you okay with that?"

I bend so he can attach the device. Darcy has another ribbon shaped communication device in her hands that she raises to her face. "Hi, Radial!"

I smile to myself. Return the greeting. I indicate the other object Saul holds.

"A device meant only for Quantum when you see her. A special delivery from me." I nod, and eject one of the tranks in my right arm, loading Saul's *special* trank into that chamber. Lock it so I don't use it inadvertently.

I reach out and place a hand on Darcy's head. Muss her hair a little more. Her smile broadens, making me wish she could see mine.

"You need to go," Saul says. "Traffic will only get worse. We can talk more on the way."

I nod. Then run.

CHAPTER

I speed away from Saul's place, glancing back a few times in the rearview mirror. Once I think I see Darcy waving from one of the windows, but I know that can't be right. There's no way to get close enough to the windows in that place. Too much junk.

She is with me, though. In the mask, she will be here.

Within a few minutes, I reach the interstate and blend into traffic. I think of the passengers in the other cars. About the oblivious lives they live. Just going on. Trying to live within the system. To be as comfortable as the vote allows. Pleasing enough strangers and friends to survive. Believing it is good.

End it. I must end it.

What will take its place? Something better or worse? I'm uncomfortable with the question, the chaos I might cause.

I call Saul to make sure they're all right.

"I used my taps," Saul says. "Quantum knows you're gone. She's reset the vote on Darcy and I. At least, for now." A pause. "I might have encouraged that decision."

I snort and shake my head. I check the mirrors for signs of pursuit, then search the sky for drones. Any indication that Quantum is watching. So far, so good.

"That also means you should be careful," he says. "She knows you're up to something."

I pass a white van on my right. Not a collection van, but I don't miss the symbolism. My heart pounds in my chest.

I will end Quantum. I am the Mask.

"How did we get to this place?" I ask.

"Interstate five," Saul says. "The same way you got in."

I check the mirrors again. The white van exits the freeway. I exhale.

"Not what I meant," I say. "How did *we*, all of us, get to this? To VoteMAX, and Quantum, and facilities...to *this*."

He chuckles. "Unusual in your kind. All this depth. You would be a good study."

"Quantum feels the same way."

He chuckles again. "I suppose she does." He draws a long breath. "We have no government armed with power capable of contending with human passions unbridled by morality and religion."

"Quoting those papers again?"

"No, John Adams," Saul says. "He led the country in the late 1700s."

"So what does it mean?"

The city's baseball stadium comes into view on my left. It is difficult to miss—a hulking structure with a roof that slides away during good weather. It is slid back today, in anticipation of an afternoon game. I glimpse the green of the infield as I drive by.

"We got here because we stopped being good," Saul says. "A good vote, good governance, depends on a moral people. If the voters aren't good in and of themselves, the vote cannot be. Representative governance is only as good as the people involved. The vote can be twisted to whatever we desire. And when we vote for our desires, the results are...rarely beneficial."

I think back to what I've witnessed. The petty posturing of Korth. The horrors of the Lake Wash facility. People who disappeared only because they were inconvenient. I clench the steering wheel, then relax my hands again. Focus on the scenery.

North of the baseball stadium is the remains of another

arena. A hollow, white ellipsis. The seats are still present, but most are coated with growth now. Moss or grass, I'm not sure which. The stadium was built for a sport that is no longer played—voted because it was too violent. Too dangerous. They used to wear headgear too, I think. Protective gear like mine, but with only a trace of a mask. The face was visible.

Ahead is the heart of the city. Skyscrapers grow up around me. Shining buildings of grey, silver, and brown. Traffic grows denser. Occupants of other cars probably think I'm on the way home from a collection. Most don't know that we're chauffeured by drivers we've never seen.

Congestion causes me to exit later than I wanted. Too far north. I make my way west, passing ethnic districts and shopping emporiums. Crowds of people with bright bags and happy faces. I find myself on Fifth Street. I pass beneath the shadow of an elevated monorail track. I remember the raw scream the monorail used to make. The rattle and heaviness of its movement.

Those days have passed too. The rail discontinued. It will soon be replaced by a new form of travel. Still suspended, only higher. "String motion," they call it. Experimental. Low energy, high output. High speed cables. Convenient and quiet.

I turn west for a couple blocks, then south again. This could be my last tour; I want to see as much as I can. I pass a museum, a park, and a library.

Finally, I reach the section of town where—according to Saul—Quantum is located. I have to admit, it is the last place I would look. There is nothing distinctive about it. Simply another city block and another group of multistory structures.

The target building is red brick and heavily lit. Ornamented with geometric patterns. It is a stepped structure. I count at least six stories on the outside, eleven at the apex. It must've been a beautiful edifice at one time. It appears empty now. Possibly condemned.

I turn past the structure and slowly circle around it. Try to see it from all sides. "What is this place?" I ask.

"An old government building," he says. "The oldest one in the area. Goes back to the city's founding."

There are only a few pedestrians here, though it is doubtless a lovely area to walk by. The sidewalk has a number of large trees growing out of it. And though unused, it appears generally clean. I scan for guards, but I don't see any. Yet.

"That seems a little obvious," I say. "Even if it is abandoned."

Saul chuckles. "Oh, Quantum isn't *in* that building, Radial."

"She's not?" I swear. "Then why am I here?"

"Because, my good collector, she's beneath it."

CHAPTER

I find an inconspicuous place to park a couple streets over. There is a grey parking garage nearby, and another red brick building with a large sign featuring the latest baseball phenom across the street. I shrink down in my seat, but keep my eyes open.

"So there is a tunnel here somewhere?" I say. "A way to the cave she's hiding in?"

"How much Green City history do you know?" Saul asks.

A couple crosses at the intersection ahead of me, holding hands. They routinely turn and smile at each other, each intently focused. Neither are inconvenient now. A short blip of time for humans, this parity in relationships. Possible unsustainable, if it even exists.

I'm reminded of Heather. When she recovers, if she recovers, is there still a chance for us? Is that possible? And if it were, would I want that?

My heart sinks. It is all shadowed now. All coated in grease.

"What history?" I ask.

"Ancient history. The city nearly burned to the ground hundreds of years ago. That led to the leaders ordering that the streets be built a story higher than they were before. For a time, people had to climb ladders to get from sidewalk, to street, to sidewalk again. Eventually, the levels below street level were left unused, becoming a forgotten underground."

I can't imagine a computer in such a place. It must be damp, dusty. "So, you think Quantum is down there somewhere," I say. "In this underground?"

"After nearly a decade of observation, yes. Perhaps she appreciates the symbolism. The fire started beneath that same government building."

I snort. "So how do I get in?"

"That, I can't help you with," Saul says. "But I'm confident she's there. So if you can find a way beneath the city, head that direction."

"The building troubles me," I say. "I don't like that it looks abandoned. Seems like a trap."

"It would pay to be cautious. She knows—"

"Right. She knows I'm up to something."

A large, white delivery truck drives by. The plates indicate it came from one of the facilities. The nearest facility is many blocks away, north of the Space Needle. But it is currently inactive.

Curious.

I glance at my suit. "I don't like walking around like this. Even though it is quiet."

The delivery truck stops at a traffic light behind me. It turns left a street before the old government building.

"You could take the suit off." Darcy pauses. "Oh wait. You don't have clothes…"

The truck disappears from view. I check the surrounding area—the sidewalks and streets. Suspiciously quiet, even for early in the morning.

I check my mirrors. Another white van is approaching. Similar plates as the first. This is weird. "I might have something here…"

The van follows the same path as the first. I wait for it to move out of view, then exit the car. I scan the street in all directions. See nothing. No one. The shoppers and workers are many blocks away. I can hear distant city noises. Vehicle sounds. Accelerations and the honk of horns.

I bring out a monitor, release it, and direct it ahead in pursuit of the truck. When it reaches the corner, it spies the truck making another turn into an alley. I keep the monitor following, and quickly follow it.

The truck stops, and two men exit wearing brown overalls. One slides open the back of the truck, revealing rows of plastic barrels. A ramp is extended, and the men load barrels onto carts and move to a green door in the building to the north.

I reach the entrance to the alley. I wait around the corner, just out of sight. I keep the monitor as high as I can to avoid detection.

The men unlock the door and roll their loads in. The door remains open. I sprint around the corner to the back of the truck. From there, I can view where they've gone.

It's a long, white hallway. I see the trailing man inside, but now a fair way off. I urge the monitor to keep the men in sight. It enters and follows them past what appears to be a number of vacant rooms, to a ramp leading downward. Directionally, it is at a slight angle to the old government building. I describe the situation to Saul.

Darcy answers. "Uncle Saul says to follow them, Radial. He says no one has simple basements there. They are all remnants of the underground city."

"Where's Saul?" I ask.

"Restroom, I think. He's been gone a while."

"Understood." I hurry to the doorway, then follow the hallway until I reach one of the rooms the monitor revealed. It is nondescript. A storage room of some sort. Faded white walls, empty drink containers, and a few scattered waist-high boxes. The only odd item is a large wooden podium.

"Can I talk to you now?" Darcy asks.

"Please do." Her voice is like having the anti-Quantum in my mask. Soon she is singing me a song about a dog and a window. It's nice.

Ahead, the men reach a large, grey room. There is another man there, also in overalls. He looks over the barrels and waves the first delivery man ahead. The other delivery man takes his burden to the side of the room and unloads it against the wall. He turns as if to return my direction. I order the monitor into hiding and squeeze behind the podium.

A few moments later he passes me. I move forward, and tell the monitor to do the same. To pursue the other men.

I reach the room where the barrels were unloaded. It is fairly large, and the floor is smooth pavement. The walls aren't completely grey, though. In a few places red brick can be seen peeking through. Like the walls from an earlier time had been plastered over. There are heavy racks in this room as well, but all are empty.

I walk to the barrel and give it a shove. It is very heavy. Completely full. The only markings are a mixture of numbers and letters. Cataloging information. Nothing descriptive in any way. I frown and move ahead.

The monitor follows the men some distance before arriving at another large room. There, I see more racks filled with plastic barrels. There's a large machine of some sort and a lot of ductwork. Or piping or something.

Is this a false lead? I search the walls around me and notice another place where red brick breaks through. Maybe this is all to fill someone's heating unit? Or an underground water supply? I could've been mistaken about the indents on the vehicle outside.

I contemplate turning back. The places to hide here are fairly limited. I see signs of an old arched doorway that had since been filled in and painted over. Traces of a different century. A different world.

"You are in the underground now?" Saul asks, now back from his break.

"I think so," I say. "Maybe. Portions look old. Brick construction." I walk slowly ahead. Absently watching the monitor feed while talking.

"You're in it, then."

I frown. "Yes, but..." I notice another passage to my right. The doorway is arched. More traces of brick.

Ahead, the delivery man wheels the barrel to a large

bronze cylinder. A door in the cylinder opens, and the man wheels the barrel to the door and, with the help of his escort, loads it into the front of the cylinder. The door closes. They turn to come back my way.

I skirt into the side passage. It isn't a passage at all, I realize, but a long narrow room. There is little effort to disguise the brick construction here. There is a pattern of large arches all along one wall. On the opposite wall is a two-meter sign that reads: Sam's Steam Baths. No idea what that means. The sign is large enough to crouch behind, though, so I do that.

The delivery men pass my position heading back toward the exit. I decide to press forward, toward the room with the machine. And the tubes. Something strange about that. It deserves a firsthand look. I command the monitor to return, and I catch it when it draws near.

The machine room is more than I expected. It is white and very clean. Solid sealed flooring. No signs of brick here. All perfectly smooth and painted. Not a crack in the surface. Nearly everything else in the room is polished bronze. Real shiny. And strange.

Along one side—my left side as I face the cylinder—is something unusual. It isn't a storage rack, as I'd surmised from the monitor images. It is more of an active loading device. The barrels get lifted up to the rack from the cylinder, turned, and placed end-wise. Then they slowly move along the rack on a conveyor to a large storage tank near the ceiling. From there the barrels roll down to a place where they are apparently emptied into the tank. The empty barrels are then transported via hooks and another conveyor to a rack on the other side of the room. There are over a dozen barrels on each side.

Exiting the large tank is a stretch of winding pipe. It snakes along the ceiling until it disappears through the far wall. There is a closed access door on that wall.

I want to study the room in more detail, but I'm concerned about the men returning with another load. I quickly describe it to Saul and Darcy, but I get only reflective mutterings in response.

"You should follow that pipe," Saul says finally.

"Yes," I say. "But first…" I release a monitor to watch the entrance, then walk to the rack of empty barrels. The bottom row is at the level of my waist. I pull out my laser burner and slowly work the triangular device over the nearest barrel's side.

So far, no sign of the men. I manage to make a square cut in the barrel's surface, large enough for me to force a gloved hand inside. I reach all the way to the bottom, fish around with my forefinger, and pull the hand back out.

My fingertip is wet with a dark fluid. I bring it up to my eyes, move it back and forth between finger and thumb.

I get a sinking feeling.

It has blood in it.

CHAPTER

I wipe my finger on the floor, disgusted. It leaves a slug-like trail of bodily fluid. I resist the urge to write the letter "Q" there, and instead stand and walk to the door on the opposite side. I try it, and find it locked. No getting Quantum to open this one. I try my decoder, and when that doesn't work, I bring out the laser burner again. I tell the others what I found.

"Sick," Darcy says.

"You need to get through that door," Saul says. "Follow that pipe."

I burn the door open, and directing my monitor a few meters in front of me, proceed on my way. This hall feels sterile. The pipe, which is still bronze, runs directly overhead. The hallway runs many meters without break or turn before angling southwest—the direction of the government building.

Ten meters later the monitor encounters another locked door. I catch up and use the decoder on that one. What follows is a series of locked doors that the decoder manages without difficulty. I worry that this might alert Quantum, but I feel like whatever I do, has to be done soon. Before my resolve runs out. I'm in dangerous territory here.

The pipe leads me around a sharp left corner. After that,

the pipe angles up into the ceiling. The hall splits, though. One hall angles left, the other right.

"I have to choose here," I say. "The pipe is gone."

"You have instruments that detect heat," Saul says. "Won't those help?"

I stare at the ceiling. It is nearly two feet over my head. My suit isn't made for leaping. Or hovering. "Not from here. Too far up." I trace the pipe back the way I came, then to where it goes into the ceiling. "Most likely path seems to be left." I send the monitor that direction. It finds a set of double doors. There is a window in one door. I bring the monitor close to that.

The room is full of guards.

I stifle a swear. Darcy is listening. "I'm going right," I say. "See where that leads."

⁂

The passage brings me to a silver elevator. It is clean and modern-looking. Equally troubling. There's a locked control next to the doors that I sweep my decoder over. No response. I hear a noise behind me and glance back. I don't see anything, but it sounded like a door opening somewhere. Possibly the door to the room of guards. Don't like that idea.

Get yourself together, Radial. You're still a mask. You could fight if you had to.

I shake my head and try the decoder again. This time a button lights up on the control. I press it and the elevator dings, then opens. I step inside.

The elevator lurches and starts going up. I don't like that either. Up is not the way I want to go. Quantum is down. Beneath the city.

The elevator stops fifteen seconds later. I brace myself, raising both arms. Tranks loaded and ready.

The doors open to a small, blue room. A reception area, complete with a desk. There's a guard at the desk—light green uniform and a badge. His eyes widen when he sees me. He jumps to his feet and his right hand drops to his hip.

I double-trank him. He gives a short yelp and collapses over the desk. I check left and right. No one else is around. Beyond the desk is a single door. To the left is another door. I approach the leftmost door first and crack it open. I see a long hallway that travels away from the government building. I close the door and sweep the room again. I only have one choice here: the door behind the desk.

I approach that and pull it open. I'm surprised again.

The room is dimly lit, large, and warm. Around the perimeter, and running in multiple rows down the center of the room, are glass canisters. Each canister stretches floor to ceiling and is approximately a meter wide. They are filled with pale, yellow fluid. Also there are—

"Did you find her?" Saul asks.

"Not yet," I say. "No." I check all my mask's sensors, especially the audio ones. The room is silent, aside from the subtle movement of fluid within the canisters.

I expect to see some sort of medical personnel here. Somebody in a white coat or a nurse's uniform.

Are they unattended? That doesn't seem right.

"So where are you? Still underground?"

I stare at the canisters, unable to fully accept what I see. I approach the nearest one and put a hand against it. It reads 95 degrees. A tad under body temperature. I'm surprised I don't see any displays anywhere. There should be something like that. Heart-rate and respiration monitors. Something.

"Radial!" Darcy says. "What is going on?"

I check the temperature of another canister, and another. "Sorry," I say. "I'm in a…a nursery, I guess. There are babies here."

"Babies?"

Floating in every canister is a tiny infant. Most seem too small to be real. All are in the fetal position, though occasionally one will twitch or move. Each has an umbilical cord attached to his or her stomach. Their cords twist upwards to disappear into the top of the canister.

The umbilicals are unsettling. Almost snake-like. As if the children are swimming with a python.

"You're in one of the gestation chambers," Saul says. "Of course…she would have one nearby."

I walk slowly down the center aisle. The infants look so similar. All are a chalky color, though there are subtle variations, mostly due to skin pigmentation.

No one carries to term anymore, I remember. Too inconvenient. Children on demand.

"Are you surprised by what you see?" Saul asks.

"I never imagined…" I touch another canister. Same temperature: 95 degrees. The difference between my readings and body temperature is probably due to the glass. Inside it is doubtless perfect.

The fluid isn't completely clear, I realize. There are tiny clumps of material suspended in it.

"Never seen a baby?"

"Not like this," I say. "No. But I meant the room. I never imagined it being like this. What did you call it? A gestation chamber?"

"You knew she needed something like this, didn't you?"

"Can you let them out?" Darcy says.

I almost laugh. "They're too small for that."

"Poor babies," she says. "Locked in a glass."

I resist tapping on a cylinder. "Safe in there," I say. "Safe and warm."

"Like a womb," Saul says. "Yes." He grows quiet for a few moments. "You need to keep moving."

I tear my eyes away and search for another door. There's one at the far end. "Right," I say. "I think I see a way out."

I get the strange perception of being watched. Not by Quantum, but by the babies under glass. That they know I'm here and why. Would they approve?

I'm doing it for them. For everyone. The future!

I jog toward the door.

^^^

The door ahead is solid metal. A complete unknown. I'm growing tired of sneaking around. Nervous. Twitchy.

Nearly two hours have passed since I left the car. Probably has a ticket by now. That won't help my vote tally.

I wrench the door open. There's a hallway beyond that curves to the right. I release a monitor and let it lead me by a couple meters. It doesn't take long to discover the hall also slopes downward.

Is this the right direction? Seems to be. Maybe.

I'm not sure Quantum is even here. This all could be a mistake. My only source of information is Saul, after all. Crazy, wounded, Saul.

Quantum was always reliable. Her information always correct. What am I following now?

I push my doubts away and move ahead. I need to see this through. I need to finish.

Soon the monitor registers something that gives me hope. A bronze pipe appearing from above. It elbows down and then bends again to parallel the ceiling, leading toward another set of double doors.

This is it. I know it.

I recall the monitor and retrieve it at a full sprint. I feel like an athlete at the end of a long competition. Tired, but also energized. Pushing through.

An alarm sounds and the hall lights begin to strobe red. The doors fly open and four men emerge. They're dressed in olive uniforms and partial armor. Two are holding green stunlashes and the others have energy rifles.

They assume a diamond formation. One man ahead, two on the sides, and one behind. They're clearly prepared. Like they were expecting me.

Expecting is one thing, but actually *encountering* a collector is something else entirely. I've caused large men to tremble. These are no different. They're armed, but worried. Conditioned to fear and obey.

I'm surprised, though. She sent only four?

"Stop there, collector!" the lead man screams. He swings his stunlash over his head and then down. Like using a garter snake to tame a lion.

I don't have time for introductions. I dive under his swing and hit him hard in the solar plexus. He falls to the floor.

The guard on the left fires a shot. I dodge, but the blast clips my right shoulder. A heavy tingle travels the length of my arm. I growl, and fire my left tranker, catching him on the chin. He screams, and joins the first on the floor.

The trailing stunlash user prepares to swing. I grab his weapon, and pulling him to me, mask-butt him. I get a tingle from that move too, but it is worth it.

The first guard starts to recover. I roundhouse him, and duck as the second energy rifle turns my way. I right trank that guard's foot. He shouts, gets a stray shot off, then begins to hop. I push him into the wall. Pound him. He falls.

Four guards on the floor. Another door ahead.

Quantum.

CHAPTER

I walk into a long, arched entranceway, and beyond that, what appears to be a vast open space. The bronze pipe angles back into the ceiling here, but I suspect that wherever it is going, it has something to do with what's ahead.

I release and engage both monitors. They move abreast at about eye level. I take in everything they give me. They enter a room of disparity. It is large, as I guessed, and circular in construction. There is a great platform in the center, and on it what appears to be a mammoth aquarium, or perhaps simply a container of some kind.

The stage looks well maintained. White. The ceiling is supported by large columns all the way around.

Completely encircling the center platform are wooden desks with chairs. The furniture is ancient. Many of the desks sit lopsided for want of legs. Some of the chairs have no legs at all. They must've been beautiful pieces of work at one time, but now their varnish is peeling off. Their stain faded.

The bronze pipe is here too. It follows the ceiling to a spot above the stage. It then angles and narrows, ending above the center of the aquarium. No fluid is coming from it, though. The aquarium is empty.

The lighting of the room is dim, save a single spotlight over the stage. It glows brightly.

What is this?

I reach the end of the entranceway and enter the room. I leave the monitors up and circling. Searching for I don't know what. The room is completely abandoned.

Is this a dead end too? A forgotten amphitheater?

I walk to one of the desks and swipe a hand across it. The dust is heavy.

I hear a loud clank, followed by a gurgling sound. A light brown fluid starts to fill the aquarium, rushing in under heavy pressure. Within minutes it is nearly full. Then a large hole opens in the aquarium's base. Something red and spongy-looking ascends into the fluid. It is at least five meters in diameter, and looks like a tumorous mass or a cyst. There are small spines on its surface.

When the mass reaches neutral buoyancy—neither rising or falling—braided lines enter the fluid from the floor. They move slowly, yet intricately, until they get to within a few centimeters of the mass. The mass's spines begin to pucker and stretch toward the lines, the cables, until they make contact. The lines are grasped and pulled into the mass, becoming part of it. It looks like a morsel of meat within a spider's web.

A larger cable falls from the pipe above into the aquarium, and joins with the mass. Whatever this thing is, the pipe is feeding it. The blood is feeding it.

It is alive, this thing. The otherworldliness unhinges me. Takes me off my course. It is living and functioning and altogether hideous.

"What do you see, Radial?" Saul asks.

"A terror," I whisper.

There's a screech of speaker feedback, and I instinctively cover my ears. It is that loud, even through the mask.

"It is good to see you again, Radial. I am Quantum. Welcome to my home."

^^^

It tortures me to hear her voice coming from the mass. A voice that I knew for so long as a friend. One that was always in my ears. Guiding me. Helping me.

She sounds as warm as ever now. As friendly. But she is a monster.

"You seem tired," Quantum says. "Exhausted. Did the guards tax you?"

I say nothing, but I am breathing hard. I *am* fatigued. Not only from the guards, but from all of it.

"I've missed you," she says. "Missed our connection. Haven't you?"

I engage my external speakers. "I'm here to stop you." I unlock the special trank and raise my right arm. "To end this. To end the vote."

There's no motion in the fluid. Not even a bubble to show that thought is happening. It is unreal, this talking to a cyst. "Do you like how I decorated?" she asks.

I scan the half-circle of empty desks and chairs, all broken and forgotten. "What is this junk?" I ask. "Why is it here?"

She mimics a laugh. "Remnants of the capital, Radial. I had them brought here after it burned. I enjoy symbols. Even you, my collector, are a symbol."

Symbols? Saul suggested as much. Guess he's not completely crazy.

"This was how decisions were made. How laws were formed. Squabbling people. Inefficient bantering. Agendas and competing philosophies often resulting in nothing. Now we have another system. True order. Me."

I shake my head. What is her game? Is she distracting me? Trying to regain my trust?

Her feeding tube twitches slightly, doubtless as more blood is drawn in. I need to focus on that. Remember that. She's using us.

"It's feeding you, isn't it?" I say. "The vote, the facilities. They produce food for you." I remember the body parts, the hanging incons. I nearly retch.

"The vote produces resources," she says. "Food if you like. But all living things require sustenance, Radial. It is a fair trade for what I provide. The services I offer."

I think of Jake, Brian, and Lanky…the people I've known that have been voted. Taken in the night. "The price is too high."

"I'm sorry you feel that way," Quantum says. "The vote is necessary. It is how PacNorth survives. It gives the people what they want. A life of convenience."

"Use what I gave you," Saul says in my mask. "Now, before it's too late."

"Do you plan to vote me?" she says. "Death in the night, do you now come for me?"

I raise my arm again. I don't care what her game is. Saul's right. It's time.

Her tube twitches. A lone bubble leaves the mass and struggles for the surface. "I'm fine with your decision, Radial. I've watched you. I trust you. But every voter should be informed. Know the consequences of his actions."

"Do it," Saul says. "Now."

I feel the weight of Saul's trank. My arm growing tired. "What do you mean *consequences*?"

"If the system ends," Quantum says, "so does civilization. Certainly you've thought of that. It will crumble."

There's truth in what she says. I've been worried about her, but in reality it is everyone else. The people casting the votes. Their choice was what brought me here.

Of course, it wasn't only them. It was me too. "We'll have to find another way." I step farther into the room, past a couple rows of desks.

She chuckles. "You saw the nursery on your way here, did you not?"

I can't forget that image. The floating infants and their umbilicals. Were they meant as symbols too? Tiny echoes of Quantum?

I nod, but say nothing.

"And you like children, don't you? You always have. Those at the SmokeHouse. Jake's son Brian. Darcy."

My arm feels heavier now. My heart aches.

"If you kill me, Radial, what do you suppose will happen to them?"

I'm stalled. I know I've brought death. But I don't want that anymore. Especially not like this. Not innocents. "Did you hear her, Saul?" I whisper.

Saul takes a long breath. "This is where voting for one's desires often leads. To situations where there are no good choices. Only the best of two evils."

"I could call a thousand guards," Quantum says. "A hundred collectors. But I won't. I know you'll do the right thing. I know you'll join me again. Work with me."

Fatigue weighs on me. My arm drops to my side. I reach for the nearest desk and lean against it. "I don't think I can do this," I say in the mask.

"After desire has conceived, it gives birth to sin," Saul says. "And sin, when it is full-grown, gives birth to death. Always death." A pause. "Another quote. The Bible that time."

"It is all death here," I whisper. "Death either way."

"What are you thinking, Radial?" Quantum says. "Why aren't you speaking to me? You had a friend, Jake. What if I could return him to you? Him and his boy?"

Jake…?

"Don't listen to that," Saul says. "She's begging. Lying."

I look at the floor. Clench my fist. "Could he be alive?"

"Anything is possible. But remove your self-interest now. That's what she's appealing to."

"Radial…" Darcy's voice. Gentle and sad. "Uncle didn't want to tell you. Didn't want to distract you." She sniffs. "Heather's dead."

I draw a long breath and let it out. Lean harder against the desk. "I killed her," I say so Quantum can hear. "Because of you, I killed her."

The tube twitches and another bubble escapes. "Killed who?" she asks. "The other collector? Heather Black?" A pause. "Every war has casualties. You know this. But she was insufficient. Inconvenient."

"This thing is going to work, right?" I say to Saul. "She's in an aquarium."

"Those nanomites won't care," he says. "They're flexible."

I nod and walk resolutely forward. Raise my right hand.

This is one vote that I won't be making to please myself. To please self-interest.

"You know," Saul says. "Jefferson once said that a government big enough to give you everything you want, is big enough to take everything you have."

I keep walking. "Sounds about right."

"They will hate you," Quantum says. "They will hunt you and rend you. Despise you, even after you're dead."

I stop. Aim. Steel myself.

"Quantum," I say. "*You've* become inconvenient."

I fire.

I see a long trail of vapor, like I ignited a tiny comet. The trank flies straight and impacts the glass with a heavy thud. There is a spiderweb of cracks, but nothing more.

Quantum laughs. Confident. Still in control. Queen of an empty system.

I wait, afraid that I haven't done anything, but also afraid that I have. Afraid for the children.

Then I detect a different color in her fluid. Something swimming within the grease. The fluid begins to darken slowly, then faster and faster.

Quantum screams.

I smile.

EPILOGUE

Darcy and Saul meet me at the tower's front door. Darcy rushes forward to greet me right away, while Saul remains back in his spider-legged chair, watching from the entrance. After the hugs are over, I look at him. His hands are knitted in his lap.

"You look better than I expected." he says.

I glance down at my suit. It has changed little from when I last saw them. A little dirtier, and my mask has started to reopen. I still have most of my tranks. Except for the fatigue, I could go out again. "All in a day's work," I say.

He looks apologetic. "Listen, about Heather..."

I feel a twinge of...what? Pain? Anger? Sadness? I shake my head and look at the nearby grassy field. "Maybe we could bury her there somewhere? Seems peaceful." I look at him. "Like the way things should be. Not collected, but laid to rest."

He gives me a halfhearted smile, and looking past me, nods. "So how are things out there?"

"Somewhat chaotic. Quantum's cameras must've fed traffic control. Lots of lanes going the wrong way now. Signals that don't change."

Saul nods. "I suspect Quantum coordinated autodrive, as well."

I snort. "Maybe. I saw lots of people parking and walking. Whole streets that are now lots. Some people must never go manual."

Saul frowns uncomfortably, then works his controlpad, shifting his seat up slightly. "You've made no friends today. I've been monitoring what's left of the system. Lots of complaints over VoteMAX being down. Anger and fear that it might impact them. That not voting might affect their personal vote matrix."

I glance at the high grass, and then toward the east. I hope for a glimpse of mountains. But so far, nothing. They're hidden behind the clouds. "Quantum was right. They will hunt me."

"Only if they know you." He motions. "Be grateful for that mask."

I shake my head. "I'm not grateful," I say. "I'm a killer. So far from that good you spoke of. Mostly selfish, or worse, uncaring. They should hate me. I hate myself." I lay a hand on Darcy's head. "The babies—"

"They aren't gone yet," Saul says. "I've notified their parents. It is up to them now. On them. Not you."

He adjusts his spectacles, then rubs his nose. "Ultimately, they'll all thank you. I ran a few tabulations." He looks at Darcy, frowns. "Quantum was increasing the collections. Slowly, but she was increasing."

"What are you saying?"

"I'm saying that if her purpose was population control, she was doing a wonderful job."

I think of Quantum's feeding tube. The bronze pipe of blood. "Maybe she got hungry. Maybe she grew."

He shakes his head. "Not at that rate. The increase is too significant. I suspect something more. Another reason. Perhaps from the outside."

A world that we know little about. That we *should* know about.

Saul fidgets, shifting his human legs. I notice something between them and the side of his harness. A black book.

"What's that?" I ask.

He looks at the book, then lifts it out where I can see.

"This?" he says. "It is about being good. About the future, and reclaiming the past." He smiles, holds it out. "You'll like it. It has blood in it."

I take the book and look at the cover. "Holy Bible," it reads. I open it and leaf through. I notice red letters in the second half. "Is this where the blood is?"

He adjusts himself. "Yes, it is all in there. A deity who gives his blood instead of taking it." He smiles, reaches out a hand, which Darcy moves into. "Now, collector, should we have a meal? I won't make you cook!"

I chuckle. "I'd like that. But first…"

I step forward and kneel, getting down to Darcy's level.

She smiles at me. A glorious thing.

"Darcy Medal, I'm Radial Crane." I reach back, work the switch at the back of my head.

And remove my mask.

THE END

THERE ARE MORE ADVENTURES OUT THERE...

That's all of Radial's story for now, but there are more fun books to read!

If you haven't read my cyberpunk trilogy yet, there's no better time. The first book, *A Star Curiously Singing*, is free for a limited time.

Find *A Star Curiously Singing* at www.nietz.com/ASCS.htm

Or for something really different, why not try the Peril in Plain Space series? The first book, *Amish Vampires in Space*, started as a joke, but ended up being a straight up science fiction story with a generous helping of Amish society and the taste of a creature feature.

Find *Amish Vampires in Space* at www.nietz.com/AViS.htm

YOU CAN MAKE A DIFFERENCE!

Word-of-mouth marketing is the best kind. Not only does it ensure that good books get noticed, it also helps bring the right books to the people who will enjoy them most.

If this book met or exceeded your expectations in any way, please consider telling your friends and/or posting a short review.

Your help is greatly appreciated!

ABOUT THE AUTHOR

Kerry Nietz is a refugee of the software industry. He spent more than a decade of his life flipping bits, first as one of the principal developers of the database product FoxPro for the now mythical Fox Software, and then as one of Bill Gates's minions at Microsoft. He is a husband, a father, a technophile and a movie buff.

Kerry has one non-fiction book, a memoir entitled *FoxTales: Behind the Scenes at Fox Software.Amish Vampires in Space* is his fifth novel and is doubtless his most talked about. Following a close second is his cyberpunk tale, *A Star Curiously Singing.*

If you'd like to get an e-mail alert whenever Kerry has a new book out or has a special on one of his already-released books, please sign up at www.nietz.com/EmailList.htm

ABOUT MASK

The genesis of *Mask* was nearly as troubled as Radial's life.

Following the completion of the DarkTrench Saga trilogy, I knew I wanted to do something different. Those books are cerebral works, and while there is certainly action, the solutions typically come through intellectual means. Sandfly is a guy with an implant in his head. He's going to solve a problem heuristically!

A fan challenged me to write something that was bare knuckle action from end-to-end. I thought this was the perfect time to answer that challenge…

I was intrigued by the sentiments I observed during the elections of 2008 and 2012, particularly this notion that popularity determines morality. It reminded me of the sort of theme that the great dystopian tales of my childhood explored. Stories like *Logan's Run, Soylent Green,* or even *Planet of the Apes*. Those stories also featured lots of action.

So, I set out to write an action-oriented dystopian story that touched on a big idea. I finished in six months—record time for me. The story was on the small side, but my first drafts are typically skeletal and gain meat during the editing process. I did a round of revising to produce a second draft, then sent it off to my publisher in June of 2012.

A month later, without reading it, the publisher put *Mask* on the release schedule for February of the following year.

I should mention here that my publisher was extremely overworked, and way too trusting. The operation was a small one, a micro-press really, and the schedule was notably compressed. Unlike larger publishing houses where books are locked and finished months before they release, here text changes might happen up until the day the book was sent to the printer.

While I waited for the edits on *Mask* to begin, I started working on a genre-blending idea called *Amish Vampires in Space*. I assumed editing would occur sometime between

August and November. I would switch gears whenever that happened.

Unfortunately, my editor wasn't able to get to *Mask* until mid-January of 2013. Less than a month before the release.

The editing process was tumultuous. The first thing he discovered was that the opening chapter of *Mask* was surprisingly similar to that of a book scheduled for later in the year. (But contracted earlier than mine.) Similar enough that he wanted *me* to contact the book's author to see if it was okay for *Mask* to go out as it was. (For the record, I had no idea about the other book while I was writing.) So, I contacted the other writer and got his permission.

Editing continued, but it wasn't long before another calamity hit: the editor didn't like the last third of the book. In that section I'd incorporated a twist that I thought was unique. Very sci-fi.

He felt the twist was unexpected, and detracted from the overall theme. We went back and forth for a couple days, searching for a solution. A feeling of dread crept over me. Dread and despair.

Ultimately, the editor offered three options: 1) I make extensive changes to the ending, 2) We leave things as they were and release it anyway, and 3) We postpone *Mask* until the October slot that was slated for *Amish Vampires in Space.*

I didn't like any of those options.

There wasn't much time to do the first. A matter of days, really. The second was a tossup. Maybe my original plot was fine, but maybe it wasn't. The editor's intuition had proven invaluable with my previous three novels. Why distrust him now?

The third solution was uncomfortable, because October—Halloween month—was the perfect time for *Amish Vampires in Space* to arrive. Plus, it would still mean lots of revisions on *Mask*, while trying to work on another book.

I went with option number one. I isolated myself from my family and started revising. I rewrote the ending, cutting some scenes, and moving others from the middle of the book to the end. I wrote over 14,000 words in less than four days. It was a miracle that a plot survived. Plus, those changes didn't make *Mask* grow. It still clocked in at around 55,000 words—almost exactly where it started. Still a short novel.

The editor gave me a terse attaboy and the book went out as scheduled.

Generally, the reviews were positive, but some commented on the rushed feel. One of my friends straight out asked me if I was rushed at the end. (You betcha, bub.) I had this nagging sense that the story wasn't all it could be. It certainly hadn't been a comfortable situation in which to create.

Skip ahead a few years. The rights to *Mask* reverted to me and I could do with it as I pleased.

Unfortunately, the experience of its genesis left me with an uneasy sentiment. The book felt like a failure. Like an *inconvenient.* I should re-release it, but I didn't want to with a dull ache in my chest. Especially if I was going to release the same rushed version.

I wasn't sure about changing it either. Could I fix what was broken? Should I try?

Finally, I decided to use *Mask* as the test document to learn a new tool. Author friends had been raving about the writing tool Scrivener for a while. In past attempts, I found it too different and complicated to use for new writing. But if I had an already composed manuscript to work with? Maybe it would be fine.

So I decided to kill two birds with one stone. I learned a new tool and re-sculpted a story at the same time.

The results feel right to me. Or at least more right. *

I hope you agree.

---

* And no, I didn't reinsert the twist ending I cut before. I'm saving that one for another book.

www.ingramcontent.com/pod-product-compliance
Lightning Source LLC
Chambersburg PA
CBHW032212190626
46810CB00019B/2699
9780997165838